# A Facility for Living

## Katie Forgette

A SAMUEL FRENCH ACTING EDITION

SAMUEL
FRENCH
FOUNDED 1830

SAMUELFRENCH.COM
SAMUELFRENCH-LONDON.CO.UK

## FOR PRODUCTION ENQUIRIES

### UNITED STATES AND CANADA
Info@SamuelFrench.com
1-866-598-8449

### UNITED KINGDOM AND EUROPE
Plays@SamuelFrench-London.co.uk
020-7255-4302

Each title is subject to availability from Samuel French, depending upon
country of performance. Please be aware that *A FACILITY FOR LIVING*
may not be licensed by Samuel French in your territory. Professional
and amateur producers should contact the nearest Samuel French
office or licensing partner to verify availability.

**MUSIC USE NOTE**

Licensees are solely responsible for obtaining formal written permission from copyright owners to use copyrighted music in the performance of this play and are strongly cautioned to do so. If no such permission is obtained by the licensee, then the licensee must use only original music that the licensee owns and controls. Licensees are solely responsible and liable for all music clearances and shall indemnify the copyright owners of the play(s) and their licensing agent, Samuel French, against any costs, expenses, losses and liabilities arising from the use of music by licensees. Please contact the appropriate music licensing authority in your territory for the rights to any incidental music.

**IMPORTANT BILLING AND CREDIT REQUIREMENTS**

If you have obtained performance rights to this title, please refer to your licensing agreement for important billing and credit requirements.

*A FACILITY FOR LIVING* was first produced under the title "ASSISTED LIVING" at ACT Theatre(Kurt Beattie, Artistic Director, Carlo Scandiuzzi, Executive Director), in Seattle, Washington, on April 19, 2013. The performance was directed by R. Hamilton Wright, with sets by Martin Christoffel, costumes by Catherine Hunt, lighting by Rick Paulsen, sound by Brendan Patrick Hogan, and props by Marne Cohen-Vance. The Production Stage Manager was Erin B. Zatloka. The cast was as follows:

| | |
|---|---|
| **JOE TAYLOR** | Kurt Beattie |
| **NURSE CLAUDIA** | Julie Briskman |
| **KEVIN** | Tim Gouran |
| **MITZI KRAMER** | Laura Kenny |
| **BEATRICE "JUDY" HART** | Marianne Owen |
| **WALLY CARMICHAEL** | Jeff Steitzer |

The mark ASSISTED LIVING was used with the permission of Compton & Bennett, Inc. (www.comptonandbennett.com).

# CHARACTERS

**KEVIN** – (25–35) aspirations exceed opportunities
and perhaps intellect. Tattoos.

**BEATRICE "JUDY" HART** – (65+) ill, but not so that
you would necessarily notice.

**WALLY CARMICHAEL** – (65+) cranky mush-pot. Overweight.
Well hidden, but present, regard for human frailty.
(Also plays Stan from the Twilight Ward.)

**NURSE CLAUDIA** – (30–50) re-energized in her role as a nurse
now that *personal responsibility* is the new slogan in health
care. Speaks quickly and with authority. Tough love
practitioner, not sadistic.

**MITZI KRAMER** – (65+) former nurse, now resident; declining
health but not kindness. Her speech is fluid and bright.
She could very easily be mistaken for an employee at the
nursing home except for rare moments of pixilation.

**JOE TAYLOR** – (65+) loyal, tenacious.

**Note**: The actors playing **JUDY**, **WALLY**, **MITZI** and **JOE** should appear
to be at least in their mid 60's. Though older would be better. **They all
strive to appear healthy and independent rather than sinking into their
infirmities**. Any choices made concerning the characters' health should
not hinder the actors from being heard or seen.

# SETTING

SPA Facility #273

# TIME

The not-so-distant future

# AUTHOR'S NOTES

**Note**: The acronyms SPA and HIPAA should be said as words, not spelled
out.

# ACT ONE

## Scene One

*(September 23rd. Second floor of federal nursing home #273. There is a nurses' station and sitting area. Barred windows. Two archways, S.R. and S.L. that lead to the residents' rooms and elevator. Giant wall clock and "Today's date is…" sign. Squawk box. American flag. Portrait of Dick Cheney.)*

*(A song plays, something like "Help" by The Beatles, which morphs into a muzak version of the song.\**)

*(Middle of the night. An aide,* **KEVIN**, *[wearing earbuds and singing, "Viva Las Vegas"\*\*] enters wheeling an occupied, draped gurney. He lifts a rug from the floor revealing a hidden hatch marked "night deposit". He opens the hatch.)*

**KEVIN.** *(yells down the shoot)* Stan! Incoming!

**STAN.** *(yelling)* I got her!

*(As* **KEVIN** *adjusts the gurney, an arm drops down from under the sheet – a large charm bracelet on the wrist. He takes the bracelet, holds it up and jingles it, just as from the hallway we hear* "Meep! Meep! Time for your pills!" *Then a bright flash of light.* **KEVIN** *quickly pockets the bracelet and tucks the arm back under the sheet.* **KEVIN** *lifts the gurney platform up and the sheeted deceased shoots down the hatch [making loud banging noises all the way].* "Meep! Meep!" **KEVIN** *takes off.)*

\* Please see Music Use Note on page 3
\*\* Please see Music Use Note on page 3

## Scene Two

*(October 19th.)*

**(JUDY HART** *sits, reading the newspaper.)*

**(WALLY CARMICHAEL** *waits for* **NURSE CLAUDIA** *who returns to her desk.)*

**(SQUAWK BOX** – *a Stepford Wife cheeriness:* "Join us for an informative lecture on avoiding falls and fractures, watch 'Hip, Hip, Hooray!' At 4 pm on in-house Channel 21!")

**(WALLY** *trundles over to her. He has a big belly, a full catheter bag flops at his ankle, wears faded Rolling Stones "tongue" t-shirt.)*

**WALLY.** I want to talk to you!

*(She doesn't respond. He rings the bell on his walker.)*

**CLAUDIA.** *(not looking up)* Yes.

**WALLY.** The bill for my insulin –

**CLAUDIA.** We've had this conversation, Mr. Carmichael. / That bill is your responsibility –

**WALLY.** /What? Speak up! You're mumbling.

**CLAUDIA.** THAT BILL IS YOUR RESPONSIBILITY!

**WALLY.** The hell it is! Medicare/ pays for this –

**CLAUDIA.** *(/overlapping)* There is no Medicare anymore! It's gone. Your doctor told you to lose weight or risk developing diabetes. You gained weight. You developed diabetes. Therefore, under SPA, the Senior Provision Act, your insulin is not covered and your baseball card collection will be sold at auction.

**WALLY.** ...what!?

*(CLAUDIA holds up and reads a laminated sign: Hearing aid battery.)*

I just replaced it! Here, you do it!

*(CLAUDIA shakes her head "no.")*

**CLAUDIA**. I don't do batteries!

**WALLY**. What!?

*(She holds up another sign and says: Get hearing aid serviced.)*

*(**CLAUDIA** exiting)*

**WALLY**. It's brand new! This is the *Pin Drop 2000*! State-of-the-art, not some goddam piece of crap! My son / worked overtime for two years to –

**JUDY**. *(loudly)* / Wally. WALLY!

*(**JUDY** hands him a note she's written. He reads it.)*

**WALLY**. She can't Dingell me!

**JUDY**. She will Dingell you! *(tossing him the newspaper)* Do the crossword!

*(From off we hear **MITZI KRAMER** calling:)*

**MITZI**. Mr. O'Bannion?

*(She enters, pen and small notebook in hand. She wears a cardigan very similar to **NURSE CLAUDIA**'s.)*

**MITZI**. Has anyone seen Mr. O'Bannion? *(moving on)* Judy, how are you feeling today?

**JUDY**. *(reading the newspaper)* Never better.

**MITZI**. *(writing)* Good. Spell "world" for me – backwards.

**JUDY**. D-l-r-o-w.

**MITZI**. *(checking)* Yes! May I take your pulse?

**JUDY**. I wish you would.

**MITZI**. Lovely. Wally! HOW ARE YOU?

**WALLY**. You're nuts!!

**MITZI**. *(writing)* Patient shows strong life force. Well. That covers rounds.

**JUDY**. Busy day?

**MITZI**. You have no idea.

**JUDY**. Have a seat, Mitz. You look bushed.

**MITZI**. How long have I been doing this, Judy?

**JUDY**. Long time.

**MITZI.** I should start thinking about retirement.

**JUDY.** Nonsense.

**MITZI.** How I'd miss the people, though. Wally –

*(Having fallen asleep reading, **WALLY**'s book falls to the floor.)*

**MITZI.** – Mr. Conklin, of course, Mr. Bickford, Kevin – what would he do without me?

*(**KEVIN**, the aide, appears. He wears a uniform and gloves.)*

**KEVIN.** *(to **MITZI**)* There you are.

**MITZI.** Kevin, do you need me, dear?

**KEVIN.** I always need you, sweetheart. Upsy daisy. We gotta get that diaper on you or there won't be a safe chair to sit on.

*(He begins to lead her off.)*

**MITZI.** They're so uncomfortable!

**KEVIN.** Do we want a repeat of yesterday?

**MITZI.** *(indignant)* I told you –

**KEVIN.** – the new resident came into your room –

**MITZI.** – Mr. Malick –

**KEVIN.** – and Mr. Malick had an accident –

**MITZI.** – number… *(She holds up two fingers.)* –

**KEVIN.** – you're really gonna blame this on the new guy, Mitz? –

**MITZI.** – I occasionally lose urine, but nothing else!

*(**SQUAWK BOX**: "Resident altercation, room 12! Repeat: Altercation, room 12!")*

**KEVIN.** *(overlapping, yelling off)* Bickford! Leave his moon rocks alone!

**MITZI.** *(sitting next to **JUDY**)* I'm meeting my son, Larry, for lunch – !

**KEVIN.** *(getting her back up)* You've got plenty of time, sweetheart – let's go…

*(*KEVIN *and* MITZI *start to exit.)*

MITZI. *(to* JUDY*)* If you see Mr. O'Bannion, *(taking something out of her sweater pocket)* tell him I have his salmon treats.

JUDY. Will do.

MITZI. *(looking in her hand)* These aren't salmon treats…

KEVIN. *(pushing her along)* Chop, chop, princess.

*(Elevator bong. A voice says:* "Your new home, buddy." JOE TAYLOR *in his wheelchair, suitcase in his lap, comes rolling on as if pushed with great force from offstage. He manages to stop at the nurses' desk. [During this scene,* WALLY *nods off.])*

JOE. Hello.

*(Phone rings.* CLAUDIA *picks up.)*

CLAUDIA. Second floor. No! Load him back into the pod, administer 5 cc's of Tranquilify, select medium heat/rotate! I don't want scorch marks. And, Stan, we're missing two med packs. Stan?! *(she hangs up)* Idiot. Yes?

JOE. I'm checking in.

CLAUDIA. Name?

*(phone rings)*

Second floor. This is she. What!? You tell the Congressman I do not have the staff or supplies I was promised! *(She hangs up.) (to* JOE*)* Name?

JOE. Taylor. Joseph. Joe.

CLAUDIA. *(finding his paperwork)* Taylor, Taylor, Taylor… Emphysema.

JOE. Not too bad.

CLAUDIA. Are you now or have you ever been a smoker?

JOE. I was.

CLAUDIA. You'll purchase your own oxygen. Prostate cancer. Are you incontinent?

JOE. No. Could you maybe keep your voice down? Sort of private information, you know?

**CLAUDIA.** No, I don't know. If you are referring to privacy laws contained in what was once known as HIPAA, then perhaps you are unaware that HIPAA no longer exists. If the taxpayer pays for your room and board, Sir, then the taxpayer has every right to know what he's paying for.

**JOE.** Guess I missed a few things in the I.C.U.

**CLAUDIA.** I guess you did. Name of a first-degree relative for rehoming purposes?

**JOE.** Rehoming?

**CLAUDIA.** A family member who may wish to house you?

**JOE.** No.

*(She goes back to her writing.* **WALLY** *calls out:)*

**WALLY.** Tony!

*(Then nods off again.)*

*(When* **JOE** *looks over at* **WALLY,** *he notices the barred windows.)*

What did this place used to be?

**CLAUDIA.** Excuse me?

**JOE.** This building – what was it, originally?

**CLAUDIA.** This used to be a federal penitentiary.

**JOE.** What happened to the prisoners?

**CLAUDIA.** They were outsourced to Pakistan.

**JOE.** Must be dozens of these by now.

**CLAUDIA.** We can't build them fast enough. We ran out of prisons, now we're converting abandoned textile factories and decommissioned aircraft carriers. *(seeing something on his chart)* You chose this facility?

**JOE.** I did?

**CLAUDIA.** Right here. Most patients take the SPA Facility they're assigned.

**JOE.** I had a relative nearby.

**CLAUDIA.** Uh-huh. Well, visiting hours are from 1 to 2 pm.

**JOE.** That would be visiting hour.

CLAUDIA. ...what?

JOE. One to 2 pm. That's just one hour. Singular.

CLAUDIA. I see your profession is listed as: actor. *(She says the word 'actor' as if it were 'pedophile'.)*

JOE. Yes.

CLAUDIA. You'll want to get to know Mr. Carmichael during *Chat Time.*

*(CLAUDIA picks up the mic.)*

JOE. I did stage/ mostly but I also directed –

CLAUDIA. /Kevin, report to the Nurses' Station for new admit. Kevin, to the Nurses' Station. *(back to JOE)* You'll be in Room 12, Bed 4. You'll be sharing the room with Misters Conklin, Bickford and Zulkowski. *(quickly, by rote:)* Lights out at 9 pm, lights on at 6 am. The Lounge here goes dark at 5. Any income, no matter how small, including pension, investments, inheritance, gifts of cash or check, and items that could be sold at Federal auction, will be routed through our accounting office. The government reserves the right at time of death to salvage any recyclables including gold, titanium and internal organs. All food and beverages from the outside are strictly contraband. You are responsible for your own toiletries including but not limited to: toothpaste, shampoo, soap, toilet paper, diapers, catheters, colostomy bags, artificial tears, artificial saliva and anal unguents. If you need clarification, the details of the newly enacted Senior Provision Act, or SPA, are located in a binder in the Lounge area. *(She points to a giant binder.)* Any questions?

JOE. A colostomy bag is considered a toiletry?

CLAUDIA. It is under the Senior Provision Act.

JOE. That's seems a little severe.

CLAUDIA. Why don't you take it up with President Cheney.

JOE. Dick Cheney? I thought he died.

CLAUDIA. He did. They brought him back.

*(KEVIN returns. CLAUDIA hands him the paperwork.)*

**CLAUDIA.** I'm going on break. See that this gentleman gets settled. *(She looks at her chair.)* Where's my sweater? Kevin, is Mitzi Kramer wearing my sweater again?

**KEVIN.** Uh…maybe.

**CLAUDIA.** Get it back.

**KEVIN.** Yes, sir. Mom! Ma'am!

**CLAUDIA.** I don't want Mitzi assisting you with rounds. Is that understood?

**KEVIN.** Yes.

**CLAUDIA.** If this job is too much for you, Kevin, we can always ship/ you back to –

**KEVIN.** /No, no, no, no, no! I can do it.

**CLAUDIA.** *(giving him a piece of paper)* Here. Ronald Reagan movies for Channel 21.

**KEVIN.** *(castor oil face)* Ronald Reagan, great. Hey, what about *(trying to make it sound high-brow)* offering a festival of classic automobile films starring iconic babes from the past?

**CLAUDIA.** /No. Doritos, Room 4; find the breach. *(to* **JOE***)* Welcome to SPA Facility #273, Mr. Taylor.

*(She exits.)*

**JOE.** Boy, she's something.

*(***KEVIN*** takes* **JOE***'s suitcase and starts out.)*

**KEVIN.** *(not listening)* …okay, Gramps, here's the deal: Conklin is pretty much with it, so don't piss him off, which means hands off his toupee and his moon rock collection. Bickford will eat anything and I mean *anything*, also likes to talk, if you're not into constitutional law, do not *engage* the man; Zulkowski's in a vegetative state, so perfect roommate.

**JOE.** *(passing* **JUDY***)* Hello. I'm Joe.

**JUDY.** Judy.

**JOE.** Nice to meet you.

**JUDY.** Good luck.

**JOE.** *(to* **WALLY***)* Hi, I'm Joe.

*(**WALLY** continues with the puzzle.)*

**JUDY.** Louder.

**JOE.** Hi!

**WALLY.** Who are you?!

**JOE.** Joe!

**WALLY.** Wally! Welcome to hell!

*(Blackout)*

## Scene Three

*(October 19th. Later that night.)*

*(SQUAWK BOX. Muzak interrupted by the voice-with-a-smile [except where* KEVIN*'s voice [in bold] fills in]:)*

*(SQUAWK BOX:* "Join us for Ronald Reagan cinema with this evening's in-house movie '**Viva Las Vegas**' the poignant tale of the famed Notre Dame coach starring a **totally hot Ann Margret**. Win one for the Gipper tonight on Channel 21, your only channel to cinema classics! *And your only channel!"* )

*(During the announcement,* KEVIN *wheels the gurney to the night drop. Sticking out from under the sheet is a cat's hind legs and tail. He sings, "What's New Pussycat?")*

KEVIN. (*yelling down the shoot*) Stan! Incoming!

STAN. Got it!

*(*KEVIN *exits.)*

## Scene Four

*(October 22nd.)*

*(JOE, WALLY and MITZI are staring into space. JOE uses a walker now.)*

*(SQUAWK BOX: "*You're special to us! Yes, each and every resident here at *(male robot voice)* SPA Facility #273 is special. That's why we're doing everything possible to place you with any living first-degree relative. Suddenly remember the name of a long-lost family member? Just let us know and we'll ship you – free of charge – into their loving arms!" )*

*(WALLY nods off, then abruptly snorts back to consciousness.)*

WALLY. Tony?

*(SQUAWK BOX: "Alzheimer's support group meets at 1 pm in the north lounge! Don't forget! ")*

*(JOE sips his coffee, makes a face.)*

MITZI. The coffee's different, isn't it?

JOE. Yes. What is that I'm tasting?

MITZI. Corn slurry – it's a thickener – to prevent choking.

JOE. Mmm.

MITZI. You get used to it. It's amazing what you can get used to. Excuse me.

*(MITZI reaches up under her skirt and quickly pulls off a diaper. Wads it up.)*

That's better. *(taking treats from her pocket)* Mr. O'Bannion? Someone's got a treat for you.

JOE. Is Mr. O'Bannion your cat?

MITZI. He's everyone's cat. But, lately, he's been hiding. He got into trouble with you-know-who for *(sotto voce) marking his territory.*

JOE. They do that sometimes.

**MITZI.** They do, even when they've had their balls cut off. The male of the species. Balls or no balls, they love to mark. Well, back to work. *(She looks at him.)* I'm sorry, I've forgotten your case history.

**JOE.** Oh, well, the short version is I was mugged, fought back, fell, broke my hip, surgery, infection, allergic reaction to wrong medication, ICU, drug-resistant pneumonia, back to ICU, then here. My condo was auctioned off to pay the bill.

**MITZI.** Old Testament's got nothing on you.

**JOE.** What's your story?

**MITZI.** I've always been a nurse.

**JOE.** No, I mean, how'd you get here?

**MITZI.** Oh! My gas pedal kept sticking which is how I drove into that Starbuck's – is that when I hit my head...?

**JOE.** ?????

**MITZI.** Then a raccoon infestation, electrical fire – p.s. those were not my cookies! – and voila!

*(KEVIN enters walking quickly, charting. Goes to nurses' station for supplies.)*

**JOE.** Kevin? Kevin?

*(KEVIN doesn't respond.)*

**MITZI.** *(to KEVIN)* Don't say it, I'm late for rounds. *(She gets up.)*

**KEVIN.** *(suddenly hearing her)* No! Mitzi, you can't help anymore.

**MITZI.** Why not?

**KEVIN.** Because you're a resident!

**MITZI.** I'm one of the best nurses you have.

**KEVIN.** Princess, you're great, believe me, but you-know-who says no.

**MITZI.** Kevin –

**KEVIN.** You don't want to get me into trouble, do you?

**MITZI.** No, but – what am I going to do all day?

**KEVIN**. Watch TV.

**MITZI**. There's only one channel!

**KEVIN**. *(seeing what she's wearing)* Wait a sec, is that yours? *(checking the tag)* Shit! *(taking her sweater off)* Mitz, you gotta stop taking Claudia's sweater!

**MITZI**. It's mine!

**KEVIN**. No. Yours has an M. written in Sharpie on the tag – *(He looks around and sees her sweater on another chair.)* – see? – this is yours.

*(He takes **CLAUDIA**'s and drops it. He then hands **MITZI** her sweater. As he does this – **SQUAWK BOX**: "Resident altercation, room 12! Repeat: Altercation, room 12!")*

Shit!

**JOE**. Kevin?

**KEVIN**. *(yelling off)* Bickford! Leave his moon rocks alone!

*(**KEVIN** starts to exit. **MITZI** follows and as she does she drops her sweater not far from where **KEVIN** put **CLAUDIA**'s.)*

**JOE**. Kevin?

**MITZI**. *(grabbing his arm)* Kevin, please don't relieve me of my duties –

**KEVIN**. Do you want to be sent to the first floor?

**MITZI**. God, no!

**KEVIN**. Okay then. *(He turns to leave. She takes his arm.)*

**MITZI**. *(following him)* What if I check the vegetables for bedsores?

**JOE**. Kevin?

**KEVIN**. *(stopping, grabbing her)* Don't ever call them that!

**MITZI**. That's what you call them!

*(**KEVIN** exits with **MITZI** following.)*

**KEVIN**. Sweet mother of mercy!

**MITZI**. *(overlapping)* Kevin, Kevin, they're my little cabbages…!

**JOE.** *(overlapping)* Kevin? Kevin? Kevin?! Could I speak – ?!

*(He's gone. Silence.* **WALLY** *snorts awake again.)*

**JOE.** Hi, Wally!

**WALLY.** What!?

**JOE.** How. Are. You?!

**WALLY.** I'm losing my mind and I have no means by which to end my life! That's how I am.

**JOE.** Fair enough.

*(***KEVIN*** *enters again quickly –* **MITZI** *right behind. He forgot to put* **CLAUDIA**'s *sweater on her chair. He mistakenly picks up* **MITZI**'s *and puts it on* **CLAUDIA**'s *chair – takes* **CLAUDIA**'s *and puts it around* **MITZI**'s *shoulders.)*

**MITZI.** *(mid-plead)* …it's a waste is what it is, to have/ someone who –

**KEVIN.** /Hey, hey, hey, hey, hey I think I might of seen a letter on your bed!

**MITZI.** From Larry?!

**KEVIN.** Maybe!

*(***MITZI*** *exits quickly.* **KEVIN** *gets the giant gloves he forgot.)*

**JOE.** Kevin? Excuse me, Kevin?!

**KEVIN.** It's *Quiet Time*, Gramps.

**JOE.** This'll just take a second.

**KEVIN.** Bad morning – Conklin's got the squirts. *(He starts to leave.)*

**JOE.** *(fierce)* Kevin!

**KEVIN.** What!?

**JOE.** Is there something we can do about Wally's hearing aid?

**KEVIN.** No. Myrtle's ears are cooked. Sorry. *(He starts to leave.)*

**JOE.** He said it used to work.

**KEVIN.** Yeah, then *phffftt* – nothing. *(He starts to leave.)*

**JOE**. Maybe I could try.

**KEVIN**. Look, buddy – you're new, right? – what's your name?

**JOE**. Joe Taylor.

**KEVIN**. Listen, Joe, like we tell families of the deceased – . Joe Taylor? Wait a sec, are you an actor?

**JOE**. Stage mostly/ but I also directed –

**KEVIN**. /Oh my god! You're Lash McGirr!

**JOE**. No, I'm not that actor.

**KEVIN**. Joe Taylor, star of: *Destination: Yesterday!*

**JOE**. Different Joe Taylor.

**KEVIN**. No, it's you. You look like him.

**JOE**. There is a slight resemblance, but I'm not him.

**KEVIN**. Yes, you are! Oh, man, I love that show!

**JOE**. It's a very common name –

**KEVIN**. They just had a marathon last weekend on Sci-Fi – the one with Ann Margret? Oh my freakin' god! Older? Yeah. Still juicy? Hell, yeah!

**JOE**. – I was a stage actor –

**KEVIN**. I watched all 36 episodes with only 2 pee breaks, which is a personal best for me. *(doing the promo) Travel with Lash McGirr as the hands of the clock go backwards and a third-rate thug gets a second chance to be a first-class citizen!* Hey, you know, I googled you and there's like nothing. What happened, man? Where'd you go?

**JOE**. I didn't go anywhere.

**KEVIN**. Was it a woman? It was, wasn't it? Are you in hiding? Hey, I get it. Sometimes a man's just got to go. Was it a woman? 'Cuz it's either a woman or drugs or your mom. With me it was all of 'em. So I totally get it. I'm in the business myself.

**JOE**. You're an actor?

**KEVIN**. Actor, director, writer, all around reconnaissance man.

**JOE**. Renaissance.

**KEVIN.** Yeah – my buddies and me just made the deadline for the *Under 10 Iphone Movie Contest.*

**JOE.** Congratulations.

**KEVIN.** Thanks.

**JOE.** What is that?

**KEVIN.** Movies under 10 seconds made for cell phone viewing at red lights. You know how there's always the best part of a movie, like the car chase or the sex? We make just that part the whole movie.

**JOE.** Like previews.

**KEVIN.** Only way shorter. But there is a narrative arc, I don't care what anyone says, story is king. Hey! You probably still know people, right?

(**JUDY** *enters. A gash of lipstick near her mouth and her very dark eyebrows are mid-forehead.*)

Judy! Guess who this is?

**JUDY.** Lindberg's baby.

**KEVIN.** Don't-know-who-that-is-try-again.

**JUDY.** I have no idea.

**KEVIN.** From TV.

**JUDY.** I don't watch TV.

**KEVIN.** From a-long-time-ago TV.

**JUDY.** I didn't watch it then either –

**KEVIN.** *(not hearing)* Joe Taylor! Star of: *Destination: Yesterday!*

**JOE.** I'm not him.

**KEVIN.** He's in hiding.

**JUDY.** No one will ever find you here.

**KEVIN.** I gotta tell Conklin. He'll pee himself. Love the make-up, Judy!

**JUDY.** Thanks, Nora did it.

(**KEVIN** *exits yelling:*)

**KEVIN.** Lash McGirr!

(**JUDY** *reads her paper upside down.*)

JOE. I'm not him. *(pause)* I am an actor though. *(pause)* Nothing big. *(pause)* No movies. *(pause)* Mostly stage.

JUDY. *(finally looking up)* Shakespeare?

JOE. "Why, my good Lady Disdain, are you still living?"

JUDY. "Is it possible Disdain should die when she hath such meet food to feed it as Signor Benedick?"

*(They smile.)*

Shaw?

JOE. "If I go to see your Salvation Shelter, will you come the day after to see me in my cannon works?"

JUDY. "Take care. It may end in your giving up the cannons for the sake of the Salvation Army.

JOE. "Are you sure it will not end in your giving up the Salvation Army for the sake of the cannons?"

JUDY. I flubbed my line.

JOE. No, it was me. Were you an actor?

JUDY. Teacher. Theatre Arts and International Politics.

JOE. Complimentary subjects. Excuse me, but your *(He indicates on his face.)* is a little, uh…

*(**WALLY** snorts awake. Sees **JUDY** and screams.)*

JUDY. It's me, you old fart! Keep your voice down!

*(**JUDY** takes a compact from her pocket. **WALLY** sneaks a Twinkie out of his walker.)*

They gave me drops this morning so I let my roommate do my face – Nora was an artist.

JOE. Abstract?

JUDY. That bad? *(She takes a tissue and wipes.)* Here?

JOE. Uh-huh. You don't need to wear make-up.

JUDY. No?

JOE. No. You have a great face.

JUDY. Thanks.

WALLY. Her real name is Beatrice!

JUDY. Pipe down, Myrtle!

JOE. Beatrice is a beautiful name.

JUDY. People call you Bea.

WALLY. I need my bag changed!

JUDY. Do you want to lose privileges?

WALLY. She can't Dingell me!

JUDY. She will Dingell you!

JOE. What does that mean?

(**CLAUDIA** *enters with a very scary looking tranquilizing gun in hand.*)

CLAUDIA. Could we please refrain from raising our voices? We have residents who are easily agitated.

JOE. Sorry. We'll keep it down.

CLAUDIA. Wrong. You will not talk. It is *Quiet Time.* And it will remain *Quiet Time* until it is announced that it is *Chat Time.*

(*She starts to leave.*)

JOE. You can't do that.

JUDY. Joe –

CLAUDIA. Excuse me?

JOE. We have a right to talk to each other.

CLAUDIA. I am Head Nurse of SPA Facility #273 and no one has a right to anything that I don't personally approve. This room is for reading and contemplation unless otherwise posted.

WALLY. I need my bag changed!

CLAUDIA. CHANGE IT YOURSELF! (*taking a breath*) Your prostate cancer has not incapacitated you, Mr. Carmichael.

WALLY. What? – you're mumbling!

(**CLAUDIA** *squints, sees something.*)

CLAUDIA. (*pointing at him*) Have you been eating Twinkies?

WALLY. (*licking his lips*) What!?

CLAUDIA. Give me the Twinkie!!

*(There is a struggle for the Twinkie.)*

**WALLY**. What Twinkie!?

**CLAUDIA**. GIVE ME THE TWINKIE – GIVE ME THE TWINKIE!

*(**CLAUDIA** holds up the, now, smashed Twinkie in its cellophane.)*

You are killing yourself and bankrupting your country!

**JOE**. It's just a Twinkie! Cut the guy some slack, he's miserable.

**CLAUDIA**. We're all miserable, Mr. Taylor! At the end of my shift all I want to do is curl up with a bottle of merlot and watch crap TV until I lose consciousness. But I don't.

**JOE**. He can't alter the way he's been eating overnight –

**JUDY**. *(overlapping) (trying to stop him)* Joe –

**JOE**. – that's a radical change!/ He needs time –

**CLAUDIA**. /No, amputating a foot is a radical change! Going blind is a radical change! And that, Sir, is his future. *(to **JUDY**)* Please communicate to Mr. Carmichael that if he receives one more diabetic demerit he will be reassigned to the first floor.

**JUDY**. I'll do that.

*(SQUAWK BOX:* "Quiet Time ending. Welcome to Chat Time!"*)*

**JOE**. I guess we can talk now, right?

**CLAUDIA**. You're new, Mr. Taylor. I would advise that you not fall in with the wrong crowd.

*(**CLAUDIA** looks at him for a moment – then exits out of the ward.)*

**WALLY**. *(overlapping)* ATTICA! ATTICA! ATTICA!

**JUDY**. *(overlapping)* Shut up! Shut up!!

*(**WALLY** takes a Twinkie out of his other pocket, smiles and puts it away again.)*

**JOE**. Kind of convenient that *Chat Time* is when she takes her lunch.

**JUDY**. She doesn't like noise.

**JOE**. That's crazy. We live here. We're going to make noise.

**JUDY**. You don't want to make her angry – her nephew works at the White House – that's him.

*(She points to a picture across the room.)*

*(MITZI enters.)*

**MITZI**. I couldn't find any letter,/I looked everywhere –

**JUDY**. / Have a seat, Mitz.

**MITZI**. Kevin thought there was a letter from Larry.

**JUDY**. Mitzi's son is a pharmacist.

**JOE**. Good profession.

**MITZI**. Especially now. The baby boomers are flooding the market – and I mean "flooding" – but I'm not one to talk. Mr. O'Bannion?

*(MITZI takes the treats from her pocket.)*

**JOE**. *(to JUDY)* What happens if Claudia gets angry?

**MITZI**. These aren't salmon treats.

**JOE**. Wait – what are those?

*(MITZI hands JOE the zip locked bag filled with small metal objects.)*

**MITZI**. I know they're finding heavy metals in fish, but – uh-oh…

*(MITZI looks at her sweater.)*

…wrong sweater.

**JUDY**. And she doesn't do hearing aid batteries…

**MITZI**. Let's put them back.

**JOE**. No. Wally! (pointing to his ear) Give me your hearing aid!

*(JOE swaps out the battery – with JUDY's help.)*

*(to JUDY)* I feel like we're in *The Miracle Worker*.

**JUDY**. I forget, does that have a happy ending?

*(They pass the hearing aid to **WALLY**.)*

**MITZI**. This is very exciting!

**JOE**. *(to **WALLY**)* Anything?

*(**WALLY** shakes his head.)*

**WALLY**. *(loudly)* Nothing.

**JOE**. Damn.

**WALLY**. Wait! Forgot to turn it on!

*(**WALLY** turns it on, looks at **JOE**.)*

**JOE**. "An asylum for the sane would be empty in America."

**WALLY**. *(normal volume)* Nothing…is as beautiful as the human voice.

**JUDY & MITZI**. Wally!

**WALLY**. *(lifting his arms)* Carmichael is back! *(wincing)* Ow!! Shit, my shoulder!

**MITZI**. I'm not going to feed these to Mr. O'Bannion.

**JUDY**. I guess that was one way to shut you up.

**JOE**. What do you mean?

**JUDY**. When Wally could hear, he'd go at Claudia for 20, 30 minutes at a time.

**WALLY**. I had every right!

**JUDY**. No one's disputing you/ had a case, Wally –

**WALLY**. /"No talking during *Quiet Time*; no alcohol; no junk food; lights on at 6 am." I didn't get up at 6 am when I was a baby! And what about you?! *(to **JOE**)* She was just as bad! *(to **JUDY**)* Agitator! *(to **JOE**)* She gave up.

**JUDY**. We've seen what happens to troublemakers.

**JOE**. What happens?

**JUDY**. They disappear.

**MITZI**. Mr. O'Bannion!

**JUDY**. Wally! You've got to promise to lay off!

**WALLY**. This is America, sister! I call it like I see it.

**JUDY**. You'll call yourself right down to the first floor!

**JOE.** What's on the first floor?

**JUDY.** The Psych Unit.

**JOE.** So they do an evaluation and send you back.

   (**JUDY**, **MITZI** and **WALLY** *laugh.*)

**MITZI.** No one ever comes back from the first floor.

**JUDY.** It's called the Twilight Ward. Everyone's sedated.

**MITZI.** They put you in a kind of heated hotdog bun and you're slowly rotated.

**JUDY.** I'll bet you're on the waiting list.

**WALLY.** Let her try!

**MITZI.** No, the rule clearly states: "Resident must pose danger to SPA property or human life." In that order.

**WALLY.** I don't care – I'm going to make her pay. / I can feel my fingers around her neck –

**JOE.** /Wally, Wally, I'd play this a little differently if I were you.

**WALLY.** Meaning?

**JOE.** You're in the catbird seat now.

**WALLY.** How?

**JOE.** She doesn't know you know – you can use that to your advantage.

**JUDY.** Where do you put your hearing aid at night?

**WALLY.** On the nightstand.

**JUDY.** Not anymore you don't.

   (*elevator bong*)

   That might be her! Mitz, sweater!

**MITZI.** (*getting up*) Oh!

**JUDY.** Wait – batteries!

**MITZI.** Got 'em!

   (**MITZI** *goes to* **CLAUDIA**'s *chair and exchanges the two sweaters, making tiny panic noises.*)

**JUDY.** Come on, come on, come on…!

   (**MITZI** *rejoins group.*)

Sleep!

(**JUDY**, **WALLY** *and* **MITZI** *drop their heads.* **JOE** *is slightly confused.*)

(**CLAUDIA** *goes to her desk, stops, turns to look at the residents.*)

**CLAUDIA**. Everything all right in here?

(**WALLY** *snorts.*)

**JOE**. Fine! Just fine.

(*pause*)

(**CLAUDIA** *takes her sweater and exits.*)

(**JUDY** *hits* **WALLY** *with her newspaper.*)

**WALLY**. What!

**JUDY**. Shut your prune hole!

**WALLY**. She thought I was asleep!

**JUDY**. Oh, right, I forgot, the great actor can convince anyone of anything.

**WALLY**. That's right, baby.

**JUDY**. If she suspects for one minute/ that you're back –

**WALLY**. /She won't.

**MITZI**. I thought your sleeping was very authentic, Wally.

**WALLY**. Thank you, Mitzi.

**MITZ**. I'm not sure the snort was quite right though.

(**JUDY** *makes a noise.*)

**WALLY**. Sweet Jesus...

**JOE**. Wally, what kind of acting did you do?

**WALLY**. Everything. Commercials, dinner theatre, stock, (*to* **JUDY**) all *professional* contracts. I would have been on Broadway had my talent been recognized.

**JOE**. Judy, any theatre?

**JUDY**. Yes, as a matter of fact.

**WALLY**. Ushering doesn't count.

**JUDY**. Acting. Community theatre.

**JOE.** There's some wonderful amateur stuff out there.

    (**WALLY** *makes a noise.*)

**JUDY.** *(smiling at* **WALLY***)* I'm happy to hear someone finally admit that.

**JOE.** What plays?

**JUDY.** *Steel Magnolias. Noises Off. Glengarry Glen Ross.*

**WALLY.** What the hell?!

**MITZI.** Frightening language in that play.

**JUDY.** It was a gender-blind production.

**WALLY.** That is just wrong.

**JUDY.** I don't think so – we extended. If you want to tap into Ricky Roma's rage, find a post-menopausal woman.

**JOE.** We're missing a bet here. You know what we should be doing?

**MITZI.** What should we be doing?

**JOE.** Theatre.

    (**WALLY** *starts laughing.*)

**WALLY.** "Hey, Judy. Let's put on a show!

**JOE.** *(overlapping)* I'm not –

**WALLY.** "Great, Mickey, we can use the barn out back!"

**JOE.** I'm not talking about productions!

**WALLY.** What are you talking about?

**JOE.** Just, you know, reading plays.

**MITZI.** Out loud?

**JOE.** Yes.

**WALLY.** Ha!

**JUDY.** For whom?

**JOE.** For anybody.

**MITZI.** I've recently been let go, so I'm available.

**WALLY.** Look, buddy, 'preciate what you did with the hearing aid, but this project ain't going to work. *(to* **JUDY***)* Tell him.

**JUDY.** Joe, listen…

**WALLY**. Tell him!

**JUDY**. I'm trying! *(to* **JOE***)* You're over-estimating the available talent pool.

**WALLY**. Remember Helen Dingell's book club?!

**JUDY**. *(to* **WALLY***)* He's new.

**WALLY**. An unmitigated disaster!

**JOE**. I bet we could do it.

**JUDY**. We've tried, people forget when to meet, they lose the books, they get/sick –

**JOE**. /I'll need your help.

**JUDY**. You don't understand, these people are –

**WALLY**. Defective!

**JOE**. That's why I'll need help.

**JUDY**. Joe…

**JOE**. One reading, that's all…

**JUDY**. Joe…

**MITZI**. Judy, he needs you…

**JOE**. Judy, he needs you…

**WALLY**. Judy, *he needs you…*

> *(Pause.* **JUDY** *looks at* **WALLY**.*)*

**JUDY**. …oh what the hell.

**MITZI**. *(overlapping)* Yea, Judy!

**WALLY**. *(overlapping)* Are you nuts!?

**JUDY**. One Hindenburg reading, then you apologize and we never speak of it again.

**JOE**. Deal.

**WALLY**. Sucker!

**JUDY**. You have something better to do?

**WALLY**. Yes, empty my bowels.

> *(He starts to leave.)*

**JOE**. Wally, wait!

**JUDY**. Let him go.

JOE. *(rapid fire, trying to stop him)* Wally, think of this! You'll get to read all those great roles you were denied because some idiot director didn't recognize your extraordinary talent!!

*(WALLY stops. Looks over his shoulder.)*

WALLY. Such as...?

JOE. Uh, Big Daddy, Stanley Kowalski...

JUDY. *(thrown away)* Caligula...

WALLY. Hamlet?

JOE. Dear God, Hamlet! *(recovering)*... yes! You're a natural.

WALLY. So you're talking, like, a staged reading?

JOE. Exactly!

WALLY. Who's our audience going to be?

JOE. Anybody who can walk, crawl or wheel out of their room to be entertained for a couple of hours. Come on Wally, what do you say?

JUDY. Helen would do it.

MITZI. She would.

*(All three stare at WALLY. Pause.)*

WALLY. Oh, what the hell!

JOE. *(overlapping)* Atta boy!

MITZI. *(overlapping)* Yeah, Wally!

JUDY. We'll need more readers.

WALLY. I can get Heppelwhite and Malick. They owe me.

JUDY. Maybe Nora could do the make-up, make her feel part of it...?

MITZI. My roommate's in a coma, but I'll ask her.

*(KEVIN enters, unnoticed.)*

WALLY. Who's going to direct?

KEVIN. Direct what?

*(Choral freeze. Pause.)*

MITZI. ...traffic?

WALLY. Nice save, nutcake.

**KEVIN**. Come on, spill it, geezers, what's up? Lash?

**JOE**. Can we trust you, Kevin?

**KEVIN**. Maybe.

**JUDY**. There's a ringing endorsement.

**JOE**. We want to do a staged reading. Here.

**KEVIN**. News flash: she won't like that.

**JOE**. We might need you to smooth the way a little.

**KEVIN**. Ya think? *(pause)* One condition.

**JOE**. What?

**KEVIN**. You get my iphone movie to somebody in the industry.

*(pause)*

**JOE**. Okay.

**KEVIN**. Let me hear you say it, you know…

**JOE**. "Travel back in time with me, Lash McGirr!"

**KEVIN**. That is so cool. Another thing –

**WALLY**. You said one condition – !

**KEVIN**. Don't get your diaper in a twist, Myrtle – hey, you can hear!

**JUDY**. Whoops.

**KEVIN**. She's not gonna like that either.

**JOE**. What else?

**KEVIN**. I want to film it.

**WALLY**. Listen, kid –

**KEVIN**. So I'll have to have some input.

**JOE**. *(to KEVIN)* Okay.

**WALLY/JUDY**. What?!

**JOE**. We need him.

**KEVIN**. He's right. I mean, come on, just logistics and shit. Getting around, HAL, the night nurse, hello?

**JUDY**. Mr. Robot.

**JOE**. Everything by the book, huh?

**KEVIN**. No, he's a real robot.

**JUDY**. HAL, short for Halliburton After-Hours Life Support.

**MITZI**. You've seen him: "Meep, meep!"

**KEVIN**. His head is a camera – it's pretty cool.

**WALLY**. Do you have any theatre experience?

**JUDY**. Oh, for Pete's sake…

**WALLY**. What? Does he understand pace, transition, objective –

**JUDY**. Of course he doesn't – he was born 2 weeks ago!

**KEVIN**. You want those Twinkies?

**JOE**. His movie was just entered in the, uh…

**KEVIN**. *Under 10 iphone Movie Contest.*

**MITZI**. *(clapping)* Yea, Kevin!

**KEVIN**. This would be for the documentary category. The prize is double for stories about old people and cripple-types and you guys are both.

**WALLY**. What is today?

**KEVIN**. Wednesday.

**WALLY**. By Friday, you'll be OLD AND CRIPPLED!

(**SQUAWK BOX***:* "Resident altercation, Room 12! Repeat: Altercation, Room 12!")

**KEVIN**. Sweet mother…! *(exiting)* Bickford! Don't eat Conklin's toupee!!

**WALLY**. Okay, let's get this disaster started.

**JOE**. All right, how about we list some titles?

**JUDY**. Good.

**MITZI**. I'll be secretary! Ready!

**JOE**. Wally – you want to start us off?

**WALLY**. *Death of a Salesman.*

(**JUDY***'s head drops back and she makes a sound akin to a cat hocking up a fur ball.)*
What?

**JUDY**. The story of a lousy father and an even worse husband. He's a liar, a cheater and worst of all, a bore.

"Attention must be paid!" Why? The guy's a grade-A jerk.

**MITZ**. *(trying to take dictation)* You're going a little fast…

**JOE**. Just the titles.

**MITZ**. Oh.

**WALLY**. Fine. What play would miss Sarah Bernhardt like to do?

**JUDY**. Something classic, good roles for everyone… *Hedda Gabler.*

*(**WALLY** bursts out laughing.)*

**WALLY**. The story of an idle whore masquerading as a housewife – she burns the guy's manuscript, wants the pretty girl's hair and when the going gets tough – spoiler alert! – she wacks herself!

**JUDY**. All right. If we want to challenge ourselves, how about a new classic?

**WALLY**. Like…?

**JUDY**. I don't know…something by Tony Kushner?

**WALLY**. Why do you hate your audience?

**MITZI**. Could we do an unknown writer?

**JOE**. Sure.

**MITZI**. I have a script that imagines a meeting between Florence Nightingale and Clara Barton. It's called: *Make Way for Nurses!*

*(Pause. **JOE**, **WALLY** and **JUDY** stare at her.)*

**JOE**. Write it down.

**WALLY**. How about *King Lear*?

**JUDY**. You've really got a thing about lousy fathers. (*to* **JOE**) Your turn.

**JOE**. *Spoon River Anthology.*

**WALLY**. Graveside monologues…?

**MITZI**. Larry did *Spoon River* in school. He played Tom Merritt who was shot by his wife's teenage lover!

**WALLY.** I don't know, a bunch of dead people sitting around talking?

**JUDY.** You don't like being typecast?

*(**KEVIN** returns, poking his head around the corner.)*

**KEVIN.** *(quickly)* Bickford's going ape shit! She's coming back to sedate him.

*(He's gone.)*

**JOE.** We'll meet tonight after dinner!

**JUDY.** Where?!

**JOE.** Here!

*(elevator bong)*

**WALLY.** They kill the lights at 5!

**JUDY.** The diaper closet! 6 pm!

**MITZI.** Tell your roommates!

**JUDY.** Sleep!

*(All four drop their heads. **CLAUDIA** runs in, sedation gun in hand [**gun is big and scary**]. She exits. Then a moment later returns – suspicious – looks at the group.)*

**KEVIN.** *(off)* HELP!! HE'S BITING MY LEG!!

*(**CLAUDIA** exits quickly.)*

*(All four raise their heads slightly and open one eye.)*

*(Blackout)*

*(**SQUAWK BOX**: "Blaming your obesity on hypothyroidism? Think again! The vast majority of obese Americans simply consume too many calories – period. So why not take the day off from lying to yourself and join us for our morning exercise program, Robot Aerobics! with Hal the night nurse, "Meep, meep!" every morning at 5 am on Channel 21! Your only channel!")*

## Scene Five

*(November 4th.)*

*(Lights come up on* **WALLY**.*)*

*(These three readings are well done – straight, no spin.)*

**HAMLET**. To be, or not to be – that is the question:
   Whether 'tis nobler in the mind to suffer
   The slings and arrows of outrageous fortune
   Or to take arms against a sea of troubles
   And by opposing end them. To die, to sleep –
   No more – and by a sleep to say we end
   The heartache, and the thousand natural shocks
   That flesh is heir to. 'Tis a consummation
   Devoutly to be wished.
   *(Blackout)*

*(November 19th. Lights up on* **JUDY** *and* **JOE**.*)*

**ALGERNON**. You are like a pink rose, cousin Cecily.

**CECILY**. I don't think it can be right for you to talk to me
   like that. Miss Prism never says such things to me.

**ALGERNON**. Then Miss Prism is a shortsighted old lady. You
   are the prettiest girl I ever saw.

**CECILY**. Miss Prism says that all good looks are a snare.

**ALGERNON**. They are a snare that every sensible man would
   like to be caught in.

**CECILY**. I don't think I would care to catch a sensible man.
   I shouldn't know what to talk to him about.
   *(Blackout)*

*(November 26th. Lights up on* **MITZI**.*)*

**ELIZA**. Now I don't care that *(snapping her fingers)* for your
   bullying and your big talk, Henry Higgins! I'll advertise
   it in the papers that your duchess is only a flower girl
   that you taught, and that she'll teach anybody to be
   a duchess just the same in six months for a thousand
   guineas!
   *(Blackout)*

## Scene Six

*(November 27th.)*

**(SQUAWK BOX***:* "Just a friendly reminder! Any illness related to obesity or lifestyle choices will not be covered by SPA. You cause it – you pay for it! So get onboard the health wagon today! Or better yet – run alongside it! ")

**(MITZI** *sits waiting, reading a piece of paper.* **JOE** *enters.)*

**JOE.** You read beautifully last night, Mitz.

**MITZI.** People have been complimenting me all day. Oh, you were terrific, too, *(clapping)* yea, Joe!

**JOE.** Thank you.

**MITZI.** My son Larry's taking me to dinner. Funny, he used to do these little plays in school – his Thomas Edison was *incandescent* – anyway, he'd ramble on and on about it, and now I'm about to do the same thing.

**JOE.** It goes by quickly, doesn't it?

*(***MITZI** *nods.)*

**MITZI.** One minute you're holding their tiny little hand in yours and the next minute… Mr. Conklin sent me a note. May I read it to you?

**JOE.** Please.

**MITZI.** "Your performance in *Pygmalion* sent me to the moon. I will be brief: you have stolen my heart."

**JOE.** He has very good taste.

**MITZI.** Thanks. May I read Hortense Robbins in *Spoon River?* She's the one –

**JOE.** – who takes the cure at Baden Baden. Sure.

**MITZI.** You know, you don't have to give Wally all the best parts.

**JOE.** I know. Where is everybody?

*(***MITZI** *shrugs.)*

**MITZI**. Wally didn't sleep well. I heard him calling out for his son – then his girlfriend.

**JOE**. Who's that?

**MITZI**. Helen Dingell. Lovely woman. Wore a giant charm bracelet – must have had 20 charms on it. Loud as a tambourine whenever it shook and she had a tremor so... Drove you-know-who crazy.

**JOE**. What happened to Helen?

**MITZI**. Don't know. People just disappear. They never tell you anything. Helen was a pistol. Threatened to call the 1-800 number. Wally was nuts about her. He's really just an old mush-pot underneath it all.

*(**JUDY** enters.)*

**JUDY**. Sorry. Nora insisted on doing my makeup again and then I had to secretly wipe it off. What?

*(Both **MITZI** and **JOE** point and speak:)*

**MITZI & JOE**. You – sorry –

**JOE**. Go ahead.

**MITZI**. You missed part of an eyebrow.

**JUDY**. Where?

**MITZI**. *(pointing)* There.

**JUDY**. *(wiping)* Here?

**JOE**. *(pointing)* There.

**MITZI/JOE**. Got it.

*(**WALLY** appears: hair combed, scarf at his neck. He stands taller. He clears his throat to announce his presence.)*

**MITZI**. *(clapping)* Yea, Henry Higgins!

*(**JUDY** and **JOE** clap, "Bravissimo!")*

**WALLY**. Oh, stop it. *(to **MITZI**)* You were pretty good yourself.

**MITZI**. Really!?

**WALLY**. You could pick up your cues, but not bad. Let's get to work!

**JUDY**. Aren't we going to wait for the others!

**WALLY**. They're not coming. Hepplewhite's got projectile diarrhea. *(group reacts)* Malick slipped on the spatter – broke his hip. *(even stronger group reaction)*

**JOE**. Bickford's out. He mistook Conklin's toupee for a coffee cake.

**JUDY**. Nora's vertigo is back.

**JOE**. Okay. Let's start. Mitz?

> *(**MITZI** hands him her notes.)*

Good reading last night. Wally, you were on fire.

**WALLY**. Thank you, Colonel Pickering.

**JOE**. Huge audience – there must have been 10, 12 people.

**WALLY**. The diaper closet can no longer accommodate wheelchairs. It's too tight. Those people will have to walk or they're out.

**JUDY**. We can't discriminate like that.

**MITZI**. No.

**WALLY**. They're dragging us down!

**JUDY**. You were in a wheelchair when you first got here!

**MITZI**. You were, Wally.

**WALLY**. Henry Higgins uses his hands! I couldn't gesture. I kept hitting people. Also, I think someone was administering CPR during my speech in Act 5. That was very distracting.

**JOE**. All right, Mitz, write down: consider venue change. *(looking at notes)* After the reading we voted to move ahead on a group generated Christmas play. Sort of a fractured nativity tale for the grandkids. Short and fun.

**MITZI**. A variety show with singing and dancing!

**WALLY**. *(to **MITZI**)* Earth to fruitloop, what planet are you from?

**JUDY**. *(bopping him)* Wally –

**JOE**. We talked about something a little less strenuous, remember?

**MITZI**. *(happy lightbulb)* That's right!

**JOE**. We'll perform on Saturday the tenth – during *Chat Time*. Kevin's rounding up chairs – if we put the audience here *(pointing to the audience)*, we should be able to pack in quite a few people.

**MITZI**. I called Larry.

**WALLY**. *(pulling papers out)* Tony's bringing the boys.

**JUDY**. They'll love it.

**MITZI**. I'd like to play Mary Magdalene – I think she's misunderstood.

**JOE**. Writing our own script will allow us to tailor the roles to each resident.

**MITZI**. Perfect, because my roommate would like to participate but she has special needs.

*(All three stare at her.)*

**WALLY**. Your roommate's in a coma.

**MITZI**. That's the special need.

**WALLY**. *(quickly)* "God grant me the serenity to accept the/ things –

*(/* **JUDY** *bops him one.)*

*(handing script to* **JOE***)* Here.

**JOE**. What's this?

**WALLY**. Last night, you told everyone to write some scenes, so I wrote some scenes.

**JOE**. That was quick –

*(***MITZI** *pulls out some papers. Then* **JUDY** *does. Finally,* **JOE** *gets out what he's written.)*

I guess we were all up late last night.

**MITZI**. It was sort of exciting.

**WALLY**. I can't remember the last time I had a flashlight under the covers.

**JUDY**. What about your wedding night?

**WALLY**. Nice one, *Beatrice*.

**JUDY**. Thank you, *Walter*.

*(***MITZI** *hands out her scripts.)*

**MITZI.** Could we read mine? Kevin made copies.

**JOE.** Sure.

**WALLY.** Can't wait.

**JUDY.** Nice big font. What is that 18?

**MITZI.** 22!

**JUDY.** Beautiful.

**MITZI.** Joe, you read, Joseph, Mary's husband and Judy, you read, Mary, the mother of god.

**WALLY.** Hello…?

**MITZI.** I thought you could read Jesus.

**WALLY.** Oh. Okay. Sounds good.

**JUDY.** I bet it does.

**MITZI.** Mary and Joseph are saying goodbye after their first date. They're sitting together on a bench, so you two need to scoot together.

(**JOE** *and* **JUDY** *follow her directions.*)

Closer. Hold hands. Nice. Okay. Go ahead.

(*reading the scene:*)

**JOSEPH.** You know how much I love being a carpenter.

**MARY.** Yes.

**JOSEPH.** But you are so pretty, I wish I could make my living just looking at you.

**MARY.** Stop. I'm blushing.

**JOE.** (*out of character.*) It says here I –

**MITZI.** That's right, go on.

**JOE.** (*to* **JUDY**) Okay with you?

**JUDY.** Sure.

(**JOE** *kisses* **JUDY**.)

**MARY.** I'm pregnant.

**JOSEPH.** I'm a better kisser than I thought.

**MARY.** No, silly. Last night I was visited by an angel.

**JOSEPH.** Uh-huh.

**MARY.** Who told me I was to be the mother of god.

**JOSEPH**. What'd you have for dinner?

*(Nurse* **CLAUDIA** *enters. Whoever sees her first, starts coughing.)*

**JOE**. Short lunch today?

**CLAUDIA**. Having a meeting?

**JOE**. I wouldn't call it that.

**JUDY**. Neither would I.

**MITZI**. Sounds so formal: *meeting. (She laughs, then they all laugh.)* It's a funny word, isn't it?! *Meeting.*

*(***CLAUDIA*** picks up one of the scenes.)*

**CLAUDIA**. *(reading)* Mary and Joseph.

**JOE**. We're writing little stories –

**JUDY**. Christmas stories –

**MITZI**. For our grandkids –

**CLAUDIA**. Looks like a script to me.

*(***JUDY*** and ***MITZI*** speak at the same time.)*

**JUDY**. No, no, it's more like –

**MITZI**. I wouldn't call it a script exactly –

**JOE**. *(cutting them off)* Yes, it's a script, all right? *(to the others)* We're not children! We don't have to hide. *(to* **CLAUDIA***)* It's a script and we're going to perform it for our families for the holidays right here. It'll be short and sweet and we'll do it on a day when you're not here so it'll be as if it never even happened, okay?

**CLAUDIA**. *(on the boil)* Not okay. See that sign? Maximum occupancy 12. That's the Fire Marshal talking – not me.

**MITZI**. But, just this once, for our grandkids/ – we'd be extra careful and –

**CLAUDIA**. /Mitzi, you don't have any grandkids.

**MITZI**. Not yet.

**CLAUDIA**. And you're not likely to, are you?

**MITZI**. …no.

**CLAUDIA**. And why is that, Mitzi?

**JUDY.** *(to* **CLAUDIA**, *quietly)* Don't.

**MITZI.** Because…

**JUDY.** Please.

**CLAUDIA.** Because your only son, Larry, died five years ago. Isn't that right?

**MITZI.** …yes.

*(pause)*

**JOE.** That wasn't necessary.

**CLAUDIA.** In the past we confabulated with residents, Mr. Taylor. *Oh, yes, your dead wife should be here/ any minute now.*

**JOE.** /I know what the word means.

**CLAUDIA.** Current protocol is to tell the truth. Mr. Carmichael, here? He talks a lot about his son, Tony, and how caring and solicitous he is – a son who has visited his father once in the entire time Mr. Carmichael has been here. I occasionally remind him of that fact so that he doesn't get his hopes up.

*(We can see that* **WALLY** *is struggling not to respond.)*

And Beatrice? She was planning a spring trip to see her nephew when I stopped her and repeated what her doctor told her right in this very room: that she would, in all likelihood, be dead/ by –

*(***WALLY** *stands, shaking, infuriated.)*

**WALLY.** /SHUT UP!

**JUDY.** Wally, no!

**CLAUDIA.** Why, Mr. Carmichael – what big ears you have.

*(He starts to walk towards her.* **CLAUDIA** *slips her hand into her cross-body bag.)*

**WALLY.** You're not a nurse; you're a malignant tumor that's metastasized to every corner of every room on this floor. You suppress all signs of life. All signs of hope. I don't know what happened to you. Maybe you were dropped at birth; maybe you're mad because you're not pretty. I don't know and I don't care. But I'll be damned if I'm going to let you get away with it!

*(Just as* **WALLY** *gets to her,* **CLAUDIA** *presses the sedation gun to his body and pulls the trigger – the noise is loud and frightening, like a nail gun.)*

*(***WALLY*** collapses onto a seat. He remains slumped with eyes partly open, staring.)*

*(***JOE*** gets up.)*

**JOE.** You can't do that!

**CLAUDIA.** Sit down, Mr. Taylor!

*(***JOE*** takes a step toward her.)*

**JOE.** YOU CAN'T DO THAT!!

**CLAUDIA.** *(holding up the gun)* I SAID: SIT! DOWN!

*(***JOE*** freezes, sits.)*

I believe you're the cause of this mischief. Why are you here?

*(pause)*

*(***CLAUDIA*** turns to pick up the mic. As she does,* **JOE** *quickly goes to* **WALLY***, takes the hearing aid out of his ear and passes it to one of the women.)*

Kevin, report to the Nurses' Station with wheelchair. Kevin, to the Nurses' Station.

*(She bends over and looks* **WALLY** *right in the eye.)*

If you had the guts to look at the truth, you'd see I'm not the bad guy here.

**JOE.** Who is?

**CLAUDIA.** *(going slightly mad)* Mr. Carmichael has diabetes, prostate cancer and cirrhosis of the liver because he was a glutton, a smoker, and a drunk. Three residents are in vegetative states because they couldn't be bothered to buckle a seatbelt. At least half of the residents are here because they spent their lives saying, "If I want to sit on the couch, eat cheeseburgers, and die young, that's my business!" Only they don't die young – they linger for years.

CLAUDIA. (*cont.*) And underpaid schlubs like me get to wipe their butts, clean their catheters and listen to the same stories day in and day out. Who's going to be there for me when I break down, hm? The Greatest Generation ransacked Medicare and Social Security and now here come the Baby Boomers! Mr. Carmichael and his drunken, sedentary cronies sucking our government dry with their chronic preventable illnesses, but I don't dare suggest that they examine their lifestyle choices, oh, no, because if I do they're going to bring up freedom and the founding fathers and the Alamo and god knows what else, because you can't tell an American anything if it's going to interfere with him doing whatever he wants to do whenever he wants to do it!! (*recovering*) Who's the bad guy, Mr. Taylor? You tell me.

(**KEVIN** *enters with a wheelchair.*)

CLAUDIA. Take Mr. Carmichael to his room.

KEVIN. Let's go Myrtle. Upsy daisy.

CLAUDIA. Clear the lounge.

KEVIN. Party's over everybody. (*No one moves.*) Chop, chop! (*fierce*) I mean it, MOVE!

(**JOE** *and* **JUDY** *exit.* **KEVIN** *starts to wheel* **WALLY** *out.*)

CLAUDIA. (*to* **KEVIN**) Wait.

(*She checks* **WALLY**'*s ears – nothing. Then his pocket – nothing.*)

Take him.

(**KEVIN** *and* **WALLY** *exit.* **CLAUDIA** *turns around to find* **MITZI** *sitting at her desk.*)

Get up!

MITZI. What's the harm?

(**CLAUDIA** *begins to document the time and details of the incident.*)

**CLAUDIA**. It agitates the residents and sets precedent for other arbitrary events. Allowing the rules to be eaten away by small encroachments is precisely why our country is where it is today.

**MITZI**. What's most appalling is you're not a good nurse.

**CLAUDIA**. Don't bother – I've heard it. Nurse Claudius. Hannigan. Ratched. I save my sympathy for those poor bastards with Huntington's and Cystic Fibrosis – not for those who ate and drank their way to a slow death.

**MITZI**. You don't seem to understand, you're dealing with human beings – people who have lost loved ones and who are doing their best to stay on speaking terms with this world. Your message is valid, but from one nurse to another, bedside manner is half the cure. Emily Dickenson wrote: Tell the truth, but tell it slant.

**CLAUDIA**. We did "slant." Pretty please eat a vegetable and walk 30 lousy minutes a day? Didn't work. Now, get up! I need to make a call.

**MITZI**. First Floor?

**CLAUDIA**. Yes.

**MITZI**. Wally's not your biggest problem. Who do you think gave him the book on lip reading? Me. The holiday play? My idea. The vomit in your new purse? I was the one who let Mr. O'Bannion into the employee break room. And now look what I've done.

(**MITZI** *gets up and looks down.*)

I've urinated all over your special chair. And on purpose, too. That's SPA property – guess I jump to the top of the list.

(**CLAUDIA** *goes to the chair to inspect it. Furious, she hits a button on the phone. We hear ringing.*)

**CLAUDIA**. I underestimated you, Mitzi.

**MITZI**. That's all right, Claudia. I'm used to it.

(**MITZI** *exits.* **CLAUDIA** *paces. We hear:*)

**PHONE.** *Thank you for calling the Twilight Ward, where everyone is resting comfortably! If you'd like to hear this message in Spanish, move back to Mexico!*

**CLAUDIA.** *(overlapping)* Come on…come on…

**PHONE.** *Projected wait time for the next available sleeping suite is: undetermined.*

(**CLAUDIA** *makes a noise.*)

*I'm sorry, I think you said, "please reserve." Is that correct?*

**CLAUDIA.** Yes.

**PHONE.** *Now, say the name of our future guest – remember you can only reserve one suite on the waiting list at a time.*

(**CLAUDIA** *pauses for a moment. Looks off.*)

*I'm sorry, I missed that – the name of our future guest is…?*

**CLAUDIA.** Mitzi Kramer.

**PHONE.** *Your order has been successfully placed. Thank you for calling the Twilight Ward! Pleasant dreams!*

(**CLAUDIA** *looks at chair closely, reels back, then (perhaps) kicks it away from the desk – hard.*)

(**SQUAWK BOX***:* "Chat Time is now ending! Welcome to Quiet Time!")

**CLAUDIA.** *(blood curdling scream)*
AAAAHHHHHHHHHHH!!!!!!!!!!

*(A song like "Summer in the City" by The Lovin' Spoonful blasts.)*

*(Blackout)*


**End of Act One**

# ACT TWO

## Scene One

*(December 4th.)*

*(As the lights go down, we hear:* "Grandchild getting married? Congratulations! Please pass along as our free gift a copy of SELF-EUGENICS: SHOULD YOU BE REPRODUCING? Family history riddled with mental illness and low IQ's? Do we really need another cousin Timmy counting on his fingers and eating dirt? Remind the happy couple to watch for the vasectomy van in their neighborhood! Friendly reminder: genetic profiles become mandatory for all government insurance starting next year."*)*

*(Night.* **JOE** *and* **WALLY** *are in their pj's.* **JOE** *has a huge smile on his face.)*

**WALLY**. …So then this 10 year-old med student comes in and says, "It's your lucky day, Mr. Carmichael, no more urine bag!" He then proceeds to yank the catheter from my urethra like he's starting an outboard motor and…why are you smiling at me like that?

**JOE**. I've got a surprise for you.

*(***JOE*** takes out a letter.)*

**WALLY**. What's that?

**JOE**. Read it.

*(***JOE*** hands it to him.* **WALLY** *starts to read – a big smile, then he laughs – really hard.)*

**WALLY**. *(lifting his arms)* THERE IS A GOD! *(grabbing his shoulder)* Owww!

**JOE**. Shhh.

**WALLY**. *(referring to his shoulder)* I gotta remember not to do that. *(referring to the letter)* How'd you get it past her?

**JOE**. Kevin brings up the mail.

**WALLY**. We're back on! *(laughing)* Boy, oh, boy, I can't wait to see her face when we/ hand her this!

**JOE**. /No, no, no. We use this only if we need to – then she has no response time.

**WALLY**. Yes! May I keep this – please, to sustain my will to live? *(tucks it away)*

**JOE**. Guard it with your life.

*(KEVIN enters.)*

**KEVIN**. Hey.

**JOE/WALLY**. Hey.

*(KEVIN holds up his iphone – so thin it appears to be a laminated picture of an iphone.)*

**KEVIN**. Gentlemen, the iPhone 12. Sweet! Clipped it – *borrowed* it from my mom. Okay, so, here's the deal. We'll do a little Q and A, you know, like, what is it like to be old? If you've got a tearjerker story, haul it out, but keep it short – sound good?

**JOE**. Yeah.

**WALLY**. All right.

**KEVIN**. *(filming)* Action! Joe. Did you ever sleep with Ann Margret?

**JOE**. No.

**KEVIN**. Shit. Okay. Wally did that pee bag on your leg drive you bonkers?

**WALLY**. He gets Ann Margret and I get a question about my pee bag?!

**KEVIN**. Fine. Did you ever sleep with Ann Margret?

**WALLY**. No. But I thought about it!

**KEVIN**. Who didn't? Joe actually had a shot at nailing the lady.

**WALLY**. You did?

**KEVIN**. He's Lash McGirr.

**JOE**. Kevin is confused.

**WALLY**. Kid's off his nut by a mile.

**KEVIN**. *(winking)* Uh-huh.

(**JOE** *winks back.*)

Next question. What's the best part about getting old?

**WALLY**. You don't give a shit what people think!

**KEVIN**. Cool.

**JOE**. I thought this movie had to be under 60 seconds.

**KEVIN**. Director's cut. Do you ever think about sex?

**WALLY**. What kind of a question is that?

**KEVIN**. An interesting kind! I think about sex, you know, like half the day.

**WALLY**. Liar! You think about sex the whole day!

**KEVIN**. Maybe. So what?

**JOE**. We understand, Kevin.

**WALLY**. We used to, too.

**JOE**. We're not talking about just being on the prowl, my young friend. Remember, Wally?

**WALLY**. Remember, I nearly went blind. We're talking *lifestyle*, when a man just has to *express* himself, if you get what I mean.

**KEVIN**. I get it, Gramps, you're talking about self-nooky and you, my elderly friends, are looking at the king. Yesterday, I oversleep after this huge party and I can't find my car keys – they're somewhere in a sea of empties, right – so I'm looking around and I lift a sofa cushion and smiling up at me is the St. Pauli Girl, you know, that piece of Swedish yum-yum on the label?

**JOE**. German.

**KEVIN**. Yeah – I'm already 15 minutes late for work – but one thing leads to another – Mr. Happy comes out to play.

**WALLY**. Kid's stuff! Get a load of this. Summer stock. *The Diary of Anne Frank*. I played a Nazi who comes on at the end. Opening night I'm waiting to make my entrance. The wardrobe girl – this zaftig goddess – I'm talking Sophia Loren at 18 – bends over to untangle an electrical cord and, heil Hitler, I'm goose-stepping it back to the dressing room – I figure I've got at least 10 minutes – only I'm wrong. I miss my entrance. Curtain comes down. Anne Frank lives. Top that!

*(pause)*

**JOE**. Freshman year at St. Benedict's. I'm first in line for the confessional. I open the door to go in just as Father Carney comes out and says, "I've got to hit the latrine – get in there and search your soul." I go into the confessional, kneel down, bow my head in prayer, and low and behold, out of the corner of my eye I see something on the floor. It's a holy card. A portrait of the Virgin Mary. Her mouth, this little pink flower, lips slightly parted, moist, glistening –

**WALLY**. STOP!!!!!!!!!! That's disgusting!

**JOE**. You're an atheist.

**WALLY**. Doesn't matter.

**KEVIN**. My girlfriend doesn't get it.

**WALLY**. Course she doesn't.

**KEVIN**. She's like, "You have me! What do you want with yourself?"

**JOE**. You'll be grateful when you hit your 40's, Kevin – each decade takes a little more of the edge off – you think about other things.

**KEVIN**. Like what?

**JOE**. Like…in your 40's?

**WALLY**. Career.

**KEVIN**. In your 50's?

**JOE.** Gardening.

**KEVIN.** 60's?

**WALLY.** Dogs.

**KEVIN.** 70's?

*(pause)*

**JOE.** *(to WALLY)* I don't want to scare the boy.

**WALLY.** He can't handle the truth.

**KEVIN.** Fine, I'll be surprised.

**WALLY.** Oh, you'll be surprised all right!

*(JUDY and MITZI enter in their pj's.)*

**MITZI.** Here we are!

**JUDY.** *(to WALLY)* Did he tell you the news?

**WALLY.** We're back on.

**JUDY.** *(to KEVIN)* You started the interviews?

**WALLY.** You're late.

**MITZI.** My fault. Rounds.

**KEVIN.** Mitz!!

**MITZI.** I rotated a few vegetables.

**KEVIN.** Sweet Jesus –

**JUDY.** All right, all right, we're here – what are we talking about?

*(Pause. The three men look at each other.)*

Uh-huh. I taught enough teenage boys to know what that look means. Mitz – we walked in on sex talk.

**MITZI.** Nothing to be ashamed of men, perfectly healthy – *(delicately)* do you have any questions for me?

**JUDY.** Come on, what are we talking about?

**WALLY.** The subject is not pertinent to womenfolk.

**JUDY.** Says who?

**WALLY.** Have you ever gotten up from a meeting at work and gone to the men's room when you didn't need to "use" the men's room but because you were bored and out of nowhere you suddenly thought of your nephew's girlfriend?

**JUDY.** No.

**WALLY.** See?

**JUDY.** I went to the ladies' room. And it was a 22-year-old Argentinian maintenance man. I was at a teachers' conference, looked out the window and there he was, shirt off, digging a trench – must have been 95 degrees that day and the sweat ran down his chest –

**WALLY.** Okay, stop!!

**KEVIN.** She got you.

**JUDY.** Wally, women enjoy sex – right, Mitz?

**MITZI.** I like to cuddle.

**JOE.** I think the subject embarrasses Wally.

**JUDY.** The man who changed the story of Anne Frank so he could keep a date with Mary Fivefingers?

**WALLY.** Who told you that?!

**KEVIN.** Time out – let's gets back to –

*(From the corridor we hear a loud, "*Meep! Meep! Time for your pills!*" followed by a sudden bright flash.)*

Shit, it's HAL! He's early!

*("*Meep! Meep! Time for your pills!*" Flash.* **KEVIN** *looks around the corner.)*

Quick! Everybody!

*(The group gets up and waits.)*

He's going into number 8. Okay…GO, GO, GO, GO, GO, GO!!

*(***JOE, WALLY, JUDY** and **MITZI** *do their best to bolt from the room.)*

*(Blackout)*

*("*Meep! Meep!*" Flash. "*Meep! Meep!*" Flash.)*

## Scene Two

(*December 5th.*)

(**SQUAWK BOX**: "Calling all patriots! Want to do something for your country? How about taking responsibility for your health? You'll never eat another hotdog after you see our colon cancer documentary: '12 Angry Polyps.' Tonight's in-house movie on Channel 21. Your only channel!")

(**JUDY** *sits reading.* **CLAUDIA** *enters looking at a picture.* **WALLY** *enters.*)

**WALLY**. *(loud, smiling)* GOOD AFTERNOON, NURSE CLAUDIA!

**CLAUDIA**. Good afternoon, Mr. Carmichael.

(*phone rings*)

(**JOE** *and* **MITZI** *enter during the phone call – sit reading the newspaper.*)

**CLAUDIA**. *(a brisk, escalating conversation)* Second floor. Yes, Mrs. Malick. *(pause)* No, it is not covered. We've had this conversation, Mrs. Malick – your husband is dying from a constellation of ailments stemming from his obesity. All he has to do to change his prognosis is lose weight. *(pause)* Yes, he has the right to live any way he chooses, but he does not have the right to expect the taxpayer to pay for his choices. Where do you think the money comes from, Mrs. Malick? Wrong. It's comes out my paycheck. Why should I pay for the consequences of your husband's dietary choices? *(pause)* Mrs. Mal – . Mrs. Malick! Predisposition does not mean "free pass," it means "try harder"! Really? Would you like to talk about the chocolate Bundt cake we found hidden in his sock drawer?! I have residents dying of cancer who would love to be told, "follow this diet and you'll live." Now if your husband isn't capable of shutting his mouth to save his – hello?

*(She hangs up and begins looking through photographs.)*

*(**KEVIN** enters charting.)*

**CLAUDIA.** Where have you been?

**KEVIN.** Tub room. Bickford's niece is bathing him.

**CLAUDIA.** Were you assisting?

**KEVIN.** No.

**CLAUDIA.** One 2 minute, assisted shower, per week, per resident. Period.

**KEVIN.** Yeah. So freakin' sad – she has to suds up all those lumps on his chest.

**CLAUDIA.** Sooner or later we all sit down to a banquet of consequences.

**KEVIN.** He looked at me with these pleading eyes, like –

**CLAUDIA.** Kevin, his doctor pleaded with him to quit smoking. His wife pleaded with him. His niece pleaded with him. His response? "Mind your own business." And that, Sir, is my advice to you.

**KEVIN.** I know – but he seems really confused.

**CLAUDIA.** It is disingenuous to dig your own grave, jump in and then ask, "how did I get here?" What do you think this is?

*(She hands him a photograph.)*

**KEVIN.** Uh...don't know.

**CLAUDIA.** Does it look like the wheel of a walker?

**KEVIN.** Nah.

**CLAUDIA.** Really? Look. Right there. What is that?

**KEVIN.** A reflection from the window – Doug's Donuts – the neon sign. I gotta finish charting.

*(**CLAUDIA** looks over at the residents, suspicious.)*

**CLAUDIA.** Kevin.

**KEVIN.** Yeah.

**CLAUDIA.** Program HAL to shoot every two hours.

**KEVIN.** Residents complain now he's waking them up.

CLAUDIA. Every two hours. Including common area and storage.

KEVIN. You mean, like, even the diaper closet?

*(The residents all slightly lower their newspapers.)*

CLAUDIA. I mean, like, even the diaper closet.

*(Residents raise their newspapers.)*

KEVIN. Yeah. Okay.

*(He turns to go.)*

CLAUDIA. And Kevin…

KEVIN. Yeah.

CLAUDIA. Please stick to the SPA approved list of movies for Channel 21.

KEVIN. That's a lot of Ronald Reagan. I was just trying to kick it up a notch.

CLAUDIA. Don't. The descriptions of the movies don't match the titles – it confuses the residents.

KEVIN. Totally my bad, I programmed it wrong, I can fix it so –

CLAUDIA. Stick to the list!

KEVIN. Right.

CLAUDIA. Where is Mr. Carmichael getting Twinkies?

KEVIN. Uh, don't know, maybe Conklin's buddy, or Malick's family, they bring in crap. I'll look into it.

CLAUDIA. Do that.

KEVIN. Mr. Carmichael sure has settled down though, don't you think?

CLAUDIA. Yes he has.

KEVIN. I had a talk with him.

CLAUDIA. Really. What did you say?

KEVIN. I told him to, you know, settle down.

CLAUDIA. Uh-huh. You don't think that perhaps the threat of being transferred downstairs might account for the change?

KEVIN. No. It was me.

**CLAUDIA.** You don't lack for confidence, do you, Kevin?

**KEVIN.** Why would I? So, uh, maybe…?

> (**KEVIN** *stares at her.*)

**CLAUDIA.** I'll make a note in your evaluation.

**KEVIN.** Sweet!

**CLAUDIA.** Stan sent the wrong med packs.

**KEVIN.** Stan…

**CLAUDIA.** *(exiting)* Change Malick's dressing.

**KEVIN.** *(calling after her)* Got it covered. No need to worry when Kevin's on board! I'll hold down the fort!

**WALLY.** Kevin!

**WALLY/JUDY/JOE/MITZI.** *Diaper closet????!!*

**KEVIN.** Sorry!

> (**SQUAWK BOX***:* "Wound care, Room 10!")

> *(exiting)* Don't pick at it, Malick!

> (**JUDY** *bops* **WALLY** *on the head [or throws something at him].*)

**WALLY.** What!

**JUDY.** "Good afternoon, Nurse Claudia."

**WALLY.** I was being friendly!

**JUDY.** You were pushing it!

**JOE.** She's right – don't provoke her.

**WALLY.** She can't do anything. We've got this!

> (*He pulls out the letter* **JOE** *gave him.*)

**JUDY.** Put that away!

**JOE.** Hand it over.

**WALLY.** Don't take it – it's all that's keeping me alive.

> (*He stashes it in his back pocket.*)

**JOE.** All right, notes from last night.

**JUDY.** She's coming back.

**WALLY.** We've got five minutes – Mitz –

**MITZI.** Yes?

**WALLY**. I want out of the manger scene.

**MITZI**. You said you'd play Jesus.

**WALLY**. Jesus, the man, yes. Love the magic – healing that leper guy – terrific shit – but, Jesus, the newborn? No.

**JUDY**. Wally –

**WALLY**. I'm too big – it doesn't make sense!

**MITZI**. It does – you're a giant baby – your birth weight correlates to your impact on the world!

**JUDY**. People loved it at the run-thru –

**WALLY**. What are you talking about? Kevin couldn't stop laughing!

**JOE**. It's too late to recast –

**WALLY**. No, we get Mitzi's roommate. She's already shrunken and in a fetal position!

**MITZI**. She's got enough to do playing Lazarus.

**WALLY**. Speaking of which – Lazarus is dead, then he's brought back to life. Now, the lady's got the first part down great –

**JUDY**. I figured it out. Mitzi and I crouch down behind her and when you order her to rise, we slowly push her up and then, blackout.

**MITZI**. How can I do that if I'm the narrator?

**JUDY**. That's right…

**JOE**. There's another concern we should address.

**MITZI**. I'd better take notes.

*(She gets out her pad and pen.)*

**JOE**. Hepplewhite is out as Wiseman – he was transported to the hospital this morning.

**JUDY**. What happened?

**MITZI**. He had a bowel movement.

**WALLY**. So?

**MITZI**. After three weeks of not having one.

**WALLY**. *Thar she blows!*

*(**JUDY** bops **WALLY**.)*

**JOE.** That leaves us with no Wisemen.

**MITZI.** Kevin could play the Wisemen.

**JOE.** He's filming.

**JUDY.** Maybe he could do both?

**MITZI.** We could ask HAL, the night nurse!

**WALLY.** He's a robot.

**MITZI.** Exactly! The wisemen were from out of town, so they'd have accents!

**WALLY.** Sweet mother of mercy...

**JUDY.** Nora feels pretty strongly that –

**WALLY.** Your roommate is blind! There is no part for her.

**JUDY.** She's knows that! She wants to do the makeup.

**JOE.** Tell her "yes."

**WALLY.** What!

**JUDY.** Thank you. And a suggestion – I think we might want to cut some of Jesus' miracles.

**WALLY.** Are you nuts?! The kids love that crap.

**JUDY.** The show is about his birth not a compilation of his greatest hits!

**MITZI.** We are running long, Wally. I'm willing to cut my scene.

**JOE.** Let's take a look at that tonight.

**WALLY.** Conklin is running out of breath before the end of his lines.

**JUDY.** He has emphysema.

**WALLY.** Well, tell him to turn up his oxygen.

**MITZI.** It's up as high as it goes.

**WALLY.** Get him a second tank and shove another tube up his nose.

**MITZI.** I'll look into it.

**JOE.** Moving on. Reminder: do not discuss this when Nurse Claudia is on duty.

**JUDY.** Even if she did get wind of it, she doesn't know the date. And believe me, she's not about to come in on her day off to –

**MITZI**. I may need an understudy.

(*Pause. They all turn to her.*)

**WALLY**. What are you talking about?

**JUDY**. Aren't you feeling well?

**MITZI**. It's not that, it's just –

**JOE**. We all get nervous, Mitz.

**WALLY**. Stage fright comes with the territory, sweetheart – get used to it.

(**SQUAWK BOX***: "All common areas are now closed. Please return to your room to receive your dinner tray."*)

(*Lights dim. As soon as the announcement begins, they begin to exit.*)

**JUDY**. *(to* **MITZI***)* You're going to be terrific, Mitz – wait and see.

**JOE**. She's right. *(exiting next to* **MITZI***)* There's nothing to be afraid of –

**WALLY**. Hey, what's that noise during my Bethlehem scene?

**JOE**. It's Kevin – he's making the sound of the camels.

**WALLY**. Why???

**MITZI**. For ambiance.

(**JOE** *sees* **CLAUDIA** *coming.*)

**JUDY**. I like it.

**JOE**. Cheese it!!!!

(**CLAUDIA** *returns.*)

**WALLY**. HAVE A NICE EVENING, NURSE CLAUDIA!

(**WALLY** *and the others exit.* **CLAUDIA** *begins to straighten the room.*)

(**SQUAWK BOX***: "Tonight's dinner is tuna fish puree and red, white and blue gelatin cubes topped with a high-fiber, black bean ganache. Beverage: decaf coffee thickened with the kiss of corn! Enjoy!"*)

*(CLAUDIA discovers the paper WALLY left behind on his chair.)*

CLAUDIA. *(reading)* "…therefore, it is my pleasure to inform you that on the afternoon of December 10th, you may exceed the maximum occupancy of the southwest common room, second floor, SPA Facility #273. Merry Christmas! Frank Martell, City Fire Marshal."

WALLY. *(offstage)* …shit!…no, no, no, no!

*(CLAUDIA drops the letter to the floor, and hides around the corner. WALLY enters, frantic, finds the letter, exits.)*

*(CLAUDIA steps out, pushes a button on her personal cellphone. Lights fade and we hear ringing:)*

PHONE. *Thank you for calling the White House. How may I direct your call?*

## Scene Three

*(Late at night.* **JUDY** *sits alone in the lounge reading.* **JOE** *enters.)*

**JOE.** I'm sorry, ma'am, but the lounge area is closed.

**JUDY.** I was just polishing my epitaph.

**JOE.** Judy…

**JUDY.** *(holding up the book)* Spoon River.

**JOE.** Oh. Who's the lucky citizen?

**JUDY.** *(looking)* One Eugenia Todd. I like her. Who are you reading?

**JOE.** Lyman King. He has this wonderful little prophecy – it's startling and, at the same time, chillingly obvious.

**JUDY.** Ooo, I'll have to go back and read that one.

**JOE.** I didn't know you were a night-owl.

**JUDY.** I'm not – can't sleep.

**JOE.** How come?

**JUDY.** Oh nothing, really…

**JOE.** What?

**JUDY.** It's embarrassing…

**JOE.** What?

**JUDY.** …*tomorrow?*

**JOE.** Tomorrow. You're not nervous? Not the woman who played Ricky Roma.

**JUDY.** I know, it's silly.

**JOE.** No it isn't. I'm nervous, too.

**JUDY.** Really? It's just a little holiday skit, right?

**JOE.** Exactly.

**JUDY.** For a handful of people.

**JOE.** Yeah.

**JUDY.** So why am I nauseous?

**JOE.** Morning sickness?

*(***JUDY*** laughs.)*

**JUDY.** Wally on the other hand.

**JOE.** He's in his element.

**JUDY.** He's a new man, thanks to you.

**JOE.** Oh, well…

**JUDY.** And I could kill you for it.

**JOE.** You know, I was wondering, why haven't they shipped Wally off to live with his son?

**JUDY.** There's a square footage rule: Tony lives in a rented room with his kids.

**JOE.** Ah…

*(pause)*

**JOE.** How'd you get here, Judy?

**JUDY.** Helen Dingell used to say she chose the wrong parents. I, on the other hand, used to smoke. I also never took a flight of stairs if I could help it. My four food groups were cheese, sugar, scotch and cured meats. Don't tell Claudia, but she's barking up the right tree.

**JOE.** Maybe, but what a bark.

**JUDY.** My turn. Were you married, Joe?

**JOE.** Yes. Elizabeth. Fifteen years.

**JUDY.** Never remarried?

**JOE.** No one turned my head that way. You?

**JUDY.** George. Didn't last long.

**JOE.** Why not?

**JUDY.** I don't think he really…liked women.

**JOE.** That could be a problem.

**JUDY.** It was.

**JOE.** No kids?

**JUDY.** *(shaking her head)* Do you have anyone coming to the play?

**JOE.** No. My sister's gone. You?

**JUDY.** My nephew'll be here.

**JOE.** Good.

JUDY. He's 19. We had a bumpy couple of years – typical stuff, you know, the young can't imagine what it's like to be old and the old can't remember what it's like to be young.

JOE. I don't know how the generations communicate at all.

JUDY. Me neither.

JOE. What do you say to a teenage boy that's gonna make any sense to him?

JUDY. "Dinner's ready?"

*(Pause. JUDY takes a deep breath.)*

JOE. Would it help to run lines.

JUDY. Would you mind?

JOE. Ready?

JUDY. Yup.

JOSEPH. You know how much I love being a carpenter.

MARY. Yes.

JOSEPH. But you are so pretty, I wish I could make my living just looking at you.

MARY. Stop. I'm blushing.

*(JOE kisses JUDY. It lasts a little longer that it should.)*

JOE. …hello…

JUDY. …hi…

*(Pause. They look at each other.)*

*(JOE moves in to kiss her again and JUDY pulls back.)*

JUDY. The script says one kiss.

JOE. Then I shouldn't kiss you again?

JUDY. *(smiling)* No – that would be very bad.

*(He leans in and before he kisses her she says:)*

JUDY. I think it only fair to tell you, I'm living on borrowed time.

JOE. …aren't we all?

*(They kiss.)*

*(Lights fade.)*

*(Sound of phone ringing, then* **KEVIN***'s recorded anemic voice:* "Second floor, your call is important to us, leave a message. Beep. This is the twilight ward! Sleeping suite now available for:" *[In* **CLAUDIA***'s recorded voice]* "Mitzi Kramer. Pick up: December 10th. We can't wait to meet you: *[***CLAUDIA***'s voice]* Mitzi Kramer. Welcome! ")

## Scene Four

*(The day of the show – in progress. "Joy to World" is heard.\* In the dark we hear: "No, silly. Last night I was visited by an angel, who told me I was to be the Mother of God. What'd you have for dinner?")*

*(No set, minimal costumes. All have distinctive "Nora" eyebrows. Broad comedic tone – think vaudeville. Goes at a clip.)*

**NARRATOR (MITZI).** (*with flashlight under chin*) And so Joseph went to his parents with the happy news of his betrothal!

**JOSEPH (JOE).** Mom, Dad, I've met a girl!

**MOM/DAD (JUDY/WALLY).** There is a God!

**MOM.** Name?

**JOSEPH.** Mary.

**DAD.** How old?

**JOSEPH.** Fourteen.

**DAD.** A little long in the tooth, son –

**MOM.** – we'll take it, we'll take it!

**JOSEPH.** And she's pregnant.

**MOM.** Kill me now!

**DAD.** Are you trying to kill your mother?!

**JOSEPH.** It's not mine, I never touched her!

**DAD.** That's good, that's good, stick with that.

**JOSEPH.** An angel told her she was to be the mother of God.

**DAD.** Too much, keep it simple, you never touched her!

**JOSEPH.** Then I saw an angel who said –

**MOM.** He's been huffing the shellac again!!!!!

**JOSEPH.** No you don't get it!

**DAD.** Oh we get it all right!

---

\* Please see Music Use Note on page 3

**MOM**. *(taking his cane and pummeling him)* You want to see angels? I'll make you see angels!!

*(exiting)*

**JOSEPH**. Ah, ma, cut it out!

## Scene Five

*(Christmas music)*

**NARRATOR**. Months later the young couple were forced to travel a great distance until they were near exhaustion.

*(Mary and Joseph enter panting in unison. One of them rings* **WALLY***'s walker bell.)*

**INNKEEPER (WALLY)**. Good evening and welcome to the Bethlehem Desert Inn! My name is Murray – how can I help you?

**JOSEPH**. We'd like a room for the night.

**INNKEEPER**. You're kidding, right?

**JOSEPH/MARY**. No.

**INNKEEPER**. See that crush of camels over there?

*(sound of camels mating)*

**JOSEPH/MARY**. Yes.

**INNKEEPER**. I'm booked solid.

**JOSEPH**. But my wife is with child.

**INNKEEPER**. Either that or someone needs to lay off the ruggala! Sorry – mazel tov.

**MARY**. Please – anything – .

**INNKEEPER**. Look, kids, I'd love to help you out, but there ain't no room at the Inn. Farshtay?

**JOSEPH**. Listen, mister –

**INNKEEPER**. Don't give me the stink-eye, give it to Caesar Augustus – Mr. Fancy-pants, "I want a census – everybody go to your hometown" – mishegas!

*(***MARY*** faints a little.)*

**INNKEEPER**. Easy there little mama! Okay, look, there's a stable around back – it ain't much but you can use it.

**JOSEPH/MARY**. Thank you.

*(***JOSEPH*** leads **MARY** off.)*

**INNKEEPER**. Young people today, oy gevaldt!

*(Christmas music)*

## Scene Six

*("Away in a Manger" plays.)*

*(We hear the* **NARRATOR**. *"And so it was that Jesus was born in Bethlehem in the days of Herod the king.")*

*(Lights up on "The Stable."* **JOSEPH** *and* **MARY** *stand admiring "The Newborn," backs to the audience. They turn out and we see that* **WALLY** *is swaddled in a sheet in a "manger" [wheelchair].)*

**JOSEPH**. He certainly is a healthy baby.

**MARY**. Yes.

**JOSEPH**. Just listen to that cry.

*(silence)*

Just listen to that cry.

*(***JUDY*** discreetly whacks* **WALLY**. **WALLY** *cries like a little baby.)*

**MARY**. I think I hear visitors

*(knocking)*

**JOSEPH**. Come in.

*(***KEVIN*** enters as the three Wisemen. He carries a blown up surgical glove in each hand – they have drawn-on faces and each [perhaps] sports a toupee. His iphone is glued to his forehead.)*

**NARRATOR**. Behold, three Wisemen from the east.

**WISEMEN**. *(out of the left side of his mouth)* Hello. *(center)* Hello. *(right side of his mouth)* Hello.

**MARY/JOSEPH**. Hello.

**WISEMEN**. We come to pay our respects to the newborn king.

**MARY**. You are certainly welcome to. Here is the child.

*(***KEVIN*** starts laughing.)*

**WISEMEN**. Boy, he's a big one, isn't he?

*(WALLY gives KEVIN the furry eyeball.)*

**NARRATOR.** *(quickly – covering)* The three Wisemen were in awe of the baby rather than, say, laughing at the large infant.

**JOSEPH.** I see you've brought something with you.

**WISEMEN.** Huh? Oh, yeah.

*(elevator bong)*

**WISEMEN.** *(left)* I bring gold. *(center)* I bring myrrh. *(right)* I bring frankincense.

*(CLAUDIA enters, breathless and victorious.)*

**CLAUDIA.** STOP EVERYTHING!!

*(Everyone freezes. MITZI turns to the audience.)*

**NARRATOR.** And so it was that the birth of the child was beset with problems…!

**CLAUDIA.** It's over!

**JOE.** No it isn't!

**CLAUDIA.** This room is in violation of fire code.

**JOE.** Not according to the Fire Marshall. Here – *(He puts his hand in his pocket to get the letter.)*

**CLAUDIA.** You mean Mr. Frank Martell?

**JOE.** Yes.

**CLAUDIA.** He's been overridden. *(giving him her letter)* By the White House!

*(JOE reads the letter.)*

**NARRATOR.** An edict from King Herod!

**JOE.** It is from the White House.

**JUDY.** What does it say?

**CLAUDIA.** It says your party is over!

**JOE.** I think it's real.

**CLAUDIA.** It's real all right. *(to KEVIN)* Clear the lounge!

**JUDY.** Don't do this, please!

**JOE.** We'll be done in 10 minutes.

**JUDY.** Look at those kids' faces.

**CLAUDIA**. *(to* **KEVIN***)* I said: Clear the lounge!

*(***KEVIN** *suddenly pulls out the tranquilizing gun and holds it up to* **CLAUDIA***.)*

**JOE**/**JUDY**/**CLAUDIA**. Kevin!!

**NARRATOR**. More gifts from the wisemen…!

**CLAUDIA**. *(vulnerable panic)* Kevin, Kevin, Kevin, don't do this, don't do this – please! Think for a minute, think! None of this is my fault!

**JOE**. What do you call giving people hell all the time!

**CLAUDIA**. I don't give 'em hell. I just tell the truth and it feels like hell. Kevin, you know I'm right – use your brain, think! – what are you doing?!!

**KEVIN**. I'm not sure. But I'm doing it. *(to* **JOE***)* This one's for you, Lash.

*(***KEVIN** *closes his eyes as though he's about to pull the trigger.)*

**CLAUDIA**. NO!! Kevin, listen to me! This man is not your friend!

**KEVIN**. Yes, he is. He's getting me into the movie business!

**CLAUDIA**. He's a liar. He's not Joe Taylor the TV star. That Joe Taylor died. This man is a fraud. Go on – ask him.

**KEVIN**. You're not him?

**CLAUDIA**. *(to* **JOE***)* Tell the truth.

**JOE**. I told you I wasn't.

**KEVIN**. But you said, "Travel back in time with me, Lash McGirr."

**JOE**. I know – I shouldn't have done that, but we needed your help.

**CLAUDIA**. Kevin. Have I ever lied to you? *(pause)* Give me the gun.

*(***WALLY** *gets up.)*

**WALLY**. DON'T!

**NARRATOR**. The baby Jesus could no longer keep quiet!

**WALLY**. Son, every man has a moment in his life that defines him. This is yours. *(to* **CLAUDIA***)* You stole my batteries!

**CLAUDIA**. To maintain TRANQUILITY! *(She regroups.)* Kevin. Use your head. Willful insubordination, assault – those show up on your evaluation and your parole is revoked.

**JOE/JUDY/WALLY**. Parole?

**KEVIN**. Yeah.

**CLAUDIA**. You've got a lot to lose, young man.

*(***KEVIN*** starts to reconsider.)*

**JUDY**. I don't!

*(***JUDY*** puts her hand over ***KEVIN****'s and fires the gun.)*

*(***CLAUDIA*** drops to her knees.)*

**NARRATOR**. *(singing)*
FALL ON YOUR KNEES – !
*(They all fall on their knees [or attempt to].)*
OH HEAR THE ANGEL VOICES. OH NIGHT DIVINE!
*(Lights begin to fade.)*
OH, NIGHT, WHEN CHRIST WAS BORN!
*(Lights go down. In the dark we hear:)*

**JUDY**. Get her into the chair!

**MITZI**. I've got her legs!

*(Lights up on* **JOE**, **MITZI**, **WALLY** *and* **JUDY** *holding up the baby Jesus sheet – hiding* **KEVIN** *and* **CLAUDIA***.)*

**JUDY**. *(pointing to the audience)* Joe, say something!

*(***JOE*** steps forward to talk to the children and to try to distract them from what's going on with ***CLAUDIA****.)*

**JOE**. Well, kids, that's our show!

*(***WALLY*** sees Tony.)*

**WALLY**. Tony's here!

**JUDY**. Go!

**WALLY**. Tony, I'll meet you!

(**WALLY** *exits.*)

**JOE**. Wasn't that lady who came on at the end, scary? Oooooh, she sure scared Joseph!

(*A* **CHILD** *yells out [pre-recorded]:* "I love you Grandpa!")

I'm not your Grandpa, sweetie, but thank you, I love you, too! And, now, we have cookies and prune juice for everyone!!

(*wild applause and shrieking from the children [pre-recorded]*)

Let's party!!

(*Lights fade.*)

(*Christmas music and party sounds*)

(**SQUAWK BOX**: "Chat Time ending. Welcome to Quiet Time!")

## Scene Seven

*(Family and friends have gone.)*

*(**KEVIN** is pacing, frantic. All are quickly wiping off their "Nora eyebrows." **CLAUDIA** is slumped in a wheelchair – she might be draped with garland.)*

**KEVIN.** Sweet freakin' Jesus! Now what?

**JOE.** How long does that stuff last?

**KEVIN.** Hours. Oh, man, I am cooked!

**JUDY.** You didn't do it! I did!

**JOE.** She's not going to remember who did it. We can tell the authorities anything we want.

**MITZI.** I'll take the fall. I'll confess!

**KEVIN.** *(touched)* …oh, man, Mitz, you're killing me!

**MITZI.** I'm not going to be here long anyway.

**JOE.** What do you mean?

*(elevator bing)*

**MITZI.** I'm, I'm moving out.

**JUDY/KEVIN.** Where?

**MITZI.** Somewhere nearby.

*(**STAN** enters with clipboard [the actor playing **WALLY** wearing a baseball cap with fringe mullet, maybe glasses, etc.])*

**STAN.** Howdy, folks! Hey, Kev.

**KEVIN.** Hey, Stan.

**STAN.** Pick up for the Twilight Ward, uh… *(consulting his notes)* Mitzi Kramer?

*(**MITZI** steps forward.)*

**MITZI.** I'm Mitzi Kramer.

**STAN.** Ok. *(notes chart)*

*(silence)*

*(**JOE** starts to laugh. Then **JUDY** and **KEVIN**. Finally **STAN** joins in.)*

STAN. Why are we laughing?

JOE. She's Claudia, our nurse.

JUDY. *(to* MITZI*)* Will you stop with the practical jokes… Claudia!?

JOE. *(indicating* CLAUDIA*) That's* Mitzi Kramer.

STAN. What happened to her?

KEVIN. Too much holiday cheer.

STAN. You gotta pace yourself.

KEVIN. That's what I told her, but, you know, chicks.

STAN. Just like my ex. *(He starts to take her.)* Okay. Here we go. I'll get these wheels back to you.

*(He stops.)*

Hey, wait just a second.

JOE. What?

STAN. I know her. She's *(He looks at her closely.)* – she works here.

KEVIN. She thinks she does. Pretends to be a nurse. It must be in your notes.

*(*STAN *looks.)*

STAN. No. Oh! Right here, "claims to be SPA nurse."

KEVIN. When she sobers up she's gonna tell you she's Claudia.

STAN. She can tell me anything she wants!

*(They all laugh again.)*

*(stopping suddenly)* Holy crap! I've given her narcotics and shit!

*(*STAN *realizing his mistake slaps his hand over his mouth.)*

KEVIN. What!!

STAN. She's really convincing! Oh, man, if this gets on my eval they'll pull my parole. Hey – uh, folks – how about we forget what I just said?

*(*KEVIN *takes a deep breath.)*

KEVIN. Gee, I don't know.

STAN. Please? They'll send me back to Pakistan!

*(KEVIN looks at the group. They all smile and nod.)*

ALL. Merry Christmas!

STAN. Oh, man, you are good people! I owe you one. *(wheeling CLAUDIA out)* Okay, here we go, *(looking back at the group)* ... Claudia*!*

*(STAN laughs. The group laughs.)*

Happy New Year!

ALL. Happy New Year!!!

*(STAN and CLAUDIA exit.)*

KEVIN. That was close! Like that episode where Lash McGirr is – oh, that's right, you're not him.

JOE. I'm sorry, Kevin. When you thought I was somebody you started calling me Joe instead of Gramps and I liked it. But I shouldn't have said I was Lash McGirr.

*(KEVIN punches a button on the phone. Ringing.)*

KEVIN. Yeah, well, I can't exactly act all that high and mighty.

PHONE. *To replace a nurse who has inexplicably abandoned their post, press one!*

*(KEVIN presses the button.)*

*Thank you!*

*(KEVIN disconnects.)*

JOE. I did send your movie to a friend though.

KEVIN. You did?

JOE. He knows people who know people.

KEVIN. Cool.

JOE. ...who know people.

JUDY. Wally still with his son?

MITZI. Uh-huh.

**JUDY**. The look on his face when he saw his boy.

**MITZI**. Just an old mushpot.

(**WALLY** *enters, beaming. The others applaud.*)

**WALLY**. They loved it!

**MITZI**. Of course they did.

**WALLY**. Tony Jr. wants to be Jesus when he grows up. Where's Mussolini?

**KEVIN**. She's being admitted to the Twilight Ward.

**WALLY**. ANOTHER MIRACLE, YES!

(*He lifts his arms as all yell:*)

**ALL**. Don't!

**WALLY**. (*grabbing shoulder, in a strangled voice*) Totally worth it.

**MITZI**. We'll have to get her out of there.

**JUDY**. Eventually.

**WALLY**. Are you nuts!? We've got her right where we want her!

**MITZI**. That's not who you are, Wally.

**WALLY**. Yes it is!

**MITZI & JUDY**. No it isn't.

**WALLY**. (*caving a little*) We'll take a vote at the next meeting. Let the people decide!

**MITZI**. A toast! To Joe!

(*They lift their glasses.*)

From the first day you came to us, things started getting better around here. To you, my friend!

**KEVIN**. (*overlapping*) I'll second that!

**WALLY**. (*overlapping*) Hear, hear!

**JUDY**. (*overlapping*) To Joe.

(*They all drink.*)

**JOE**. Before I got here I owed all of you a huge debt of gratitude.

(**JOE** *takes a letter from his pocket.*)

KEVIN. Bong toke, man – doesn't make sense.

MITZI. He's being poetic – right, Joe?

JOE. *(reading)* "Dear Little Brother: Where the hell are you? I've called and called. Please tell me you're on tour with some wonderful play. I'm currently residing at SPA Facility #273, a mausoleum for the soon-to-be departed. Yes, I'm afraid the prognosis isn't good – not something I like putting in a letter, but I repeat, "where the hell are you?" My days are made bearable by Judy and Mitzi, two gals dad would have called "the real deal." We yammer and laugh like there's no tomorrow – and guess what? – there may not be. Judy reminds me of your Elizabeth, Joe. Then, there's a man here, Wally Carmichael and, Joe, he is so much like my Harold: irascible, pig-headed and utterly irresistible. Last night he snuck into my room, and we held hands and did the crossword puzzle. It was heaven. There's also a nurse here – one of those unhappy types. Remember Mrs. Gunther across the street? Like her. I've been giving her hell and I'm fairly certain she's going to hasten my departure by reassigning me to a place they call the Twilight Ward." This next part is sort of personal. She ends: "My love and strong intention of seeing you again in a better place – your much younger looking sister, Helen."

*(*JOE *looks up.)*

Dingell. That was her married name. "PS There's a kid here, an aide named Kevin, a lovable felon if there ever was one –

KEVIN. She thought I was lovable!

JOE. – see that he gets my charm bracelet for his girlfriend. He's had his eye on it for some time."

*(*JOE *looks up. They all look at* KEVIN.*)*

KEVIN. Done.

*(pause)*

MITZI. My goodness.

**WALLY**. She was something, your sister.

**JUDY**. She was.

**MITZI**. Wanted to know all about Larry.

**KEVIN**. That's a coincidence, you coming here.

**WALLY**. For god's sake, son, put it together.

**KEVIN**. Ohhh, like, on purpose – undercover?!

**JOE**. Little bit.

**KEVIN**. Very Lash McGirr.

(pause)

**JOE**. Do any of you know – was she in the Twilight Ward? At the end?

(Pause. They can't look at him or answer – all believing that she was.)

**KEVIN**. No, she wasn't.

**WALLY**. She wasn't…?

(All turn to **KEVIN**.)

**KEVIN**. She died before she was transferred –

**WALLY**. (whispered) Thank god…

**MITZI**. (overlapping with **WALLY**) (softly clapping) …yea, Helen…

**KEVIN**. She looked peaceful, Joe, not like some of 'em.

**JOE**. That is the best Christmas present I've ever received.

(**JOE** shakes **KEVIN**'s hand with gratitude, then his tone completely changes.)

**JOE**. Well – enough of that. Carpe diem!

**WALLY**. Hear, hear.

**JOE**. Rehearsal anyone?

**JUDY**. Great idea.

**KEVIN**. Hey, could I, maybe, you know, participate…?

**WALLY**. Son, your three Wisemen were the price of your admission.

**KEVIN**. Cool. Cuz' I was thinking maybe we could do the musical, *Hair. (singing)* "Long beautiful hair – !"

**WALLY**. You're out.

**MITZI**. Kudos for bravery!

**JUDY**. *Spoon River's* next.

**JOE**. Anyone have an epitaph?

**WALLY/JUDY/MITZI**. I do.

**JOE**. Great. Now, remember what we talked about. These people may be dead, but they've got something to say – so sell it. Wally, will you start us off?

**WALLY**. No. You start us off, Joe.

**JOE**. All right. *(He stands – looks to the booth.)* Lights!

*(A spotlight comes up on* **JOE**.*)*

Lyman King.

You may think, passer-by, that Fate
Is a pit-fall outside of yourself,
Around which you may walk by the use of foresight
And wisdom.
Thus you believe, viewing the lives of other men,
As one who in God-like fashion bends over an anthill,
Seeing how their difficulties could be avoided.
But pass on into life:
In time you shall see Fate approach you
In the shape of your own image in the mirror;
Or you shall sit alone by your own hearth,
And suddenly the chair by you shall hold a guest,
And you shall know that guest
And read the authentic message of his eyes.

*(Lights fade.)*

*(a song like, "Wouldn't It Be Nice" by The Beach Boys)*

**End of Play**